Juli Scott
Super Sleuth
Book 3

Wednesday Witness

Colleen L. Reece

D1057161

BARBOUR
PUBLISHING, INC.
Uhrichsville, OH

Wednesday Witness

Y
F
Ree

© MCMXCVIII by Barbour Publishing, Inc.

ISBN 1-57748-179-8

Published by Barbour Publishing, Inc.
P.O. Box 719
Uhrichsville, Ohio 44683
http://www.barbourbooks.com

Member of the
Evangelical Christian
Publishers Association

Printed in the United States of America.

Chapter 1

A low moaning sound dragged Juli Scott from the depths of sleep to a barely conscious state. The sixteen-year-old girl groggily peered through a tousled curtain of blondish-brown hair at her digital clock. Large red numerals glowed 4:00 A.M., the hour people in the medical profession said a person's body was at its lowest ebb. Juli yawned. Hers certainly was its low point! All she wanted to do was go back to sleep. No self-respecting high school sophomore in her right mind should be awake at such a ghastly hour.

> *We are the sophomores, mighty, mighty*
> *   sophomores.*
> *Everywhere we go-o, people want to know-oh,*
> *   Who we are.*
> *So we tell them,*
> *   WE ARE THE SOPHOMORES!*

The chant she and her classmates used in an effort to impress the lowly freshmen at Bellingham, Washington's Hillcrest High School sang through Juli's tired brain. She flopped back on her pillow. Great. The last thing she needed was having the words hammer at her in the middle of the night!

Juli curled into a question mark, hugged her cinnamon-brown teddy bear Clue, and closed her dark blue eyes. The moan came again. Weird. Usually when the wind blew off Bellingham Bay, it whistled around the corners of the Scotts' yellow ranch style house, looking for a loose white shutter or flower-filled window box to rattle.

She pulled her pillow over her head and drifted back to sleep, only to find herself wide awake and sitting straight up in bed when a third moan came, this time much closer. Her pulse raced. No howling wind had made that wailing sound, followed by the mumbled words, "Please. Let me go home."

Juli switched on her reading lamp, leapt out of bed, and ran to the second twin bed in her cozy, yellow-walled bedroom. She flung back the yellow comforter that matched the one on her own bed and shook her best friend's shoulder. "Wake up, Shannon. You're having a nightmare!"

Dark-haired Shannon Riley opened unfocused Irish blue-gray eyes. Terror clouded them and she shrank away from Juli's clutching hands. "Don't hurt me, please," she squeaked out. Then she said in a hoarse voice, "I will fear no evil: for Thou art with me."

Juli recognized the quotation as part of the 23rd Psalm. Shannon had repeated those ten words over and over while being held prisoner by the Children of Light leaders earlier in the spring. Clinging to this Scripture had helped save her sanity during the cult's brainwashing sessions. Juli shuddered. According to Dr. Marlowe, the Scotts' family doctor, Shannon's daring rescue by three of the church youth group boys had come just in time to save her life.

A basketball-size lump of pity for the fragile shadow Shannon had become parked in Juli's throat. "I'm here, Shannon. No one's going to hurt you. Not now. Not *ever*." She patted her friend's clenched fingers.

"Juli?" Awareness of her surroundings gradually replaced the fear in Shannon's face. She blinked wet dark lashes, so long they made half-moons on her white cheeks when she slept. Tears Juli knew came from sheer helplessness trickled onto her pillow. "I'm sorry I woke you."

"Don't be." Juli forced a grin to hide the ache in her heart. "What's a little lost sleep between friends?" She hesitated. "Same dream?"

"Yes." Shannon's dark head moved restlessly up and down. She licked parched lips and Juli hurried to the bathroom for a glass of water. She also brought a damp washcloth. Shannon drained the glass and wiped her sweaty face. "Thanks." She looked at the twisted bed sheets. "I guess I got all tangled up. I thought I was back at the compound." A hint of fear still lurked in the eyes that looked more gray than blue and absolutely enormous in Shannon's too-thin face. She had dropped from the 120 pounds both she and Juli normally weighed to only 105, too little for her (and Juli's) 5'7" height.

"Want to raid the fridge?" Juli impulsively asked.

"No, but thanks. Are you tryin' to put weight on my bones?"

Juli blinked. "You mean *meat* on your bones. Hey, you must be getting better. This is the first time you've misquoted anything in ages."

Some of Shannon's old sparkle returned. It tilted her sensitive lips up and brightened her face. "Mercy me, so you're for missin' my Rileyisms, are you?"

"Now I know you're better!" Juli told her in relief. "You lost most of your brogue last fall, not long after you came from Ireland." She cocked her head to one side. "Bad as I hate to admit it, I really do miss your Rileyisms. So does everyone else. Our happy principal, Mr. S. Miles—"

"Mr. *Smiles*," Shannon interrupted, recalling the popular nickname for the man.

"Uh-huh. Anyway, he said he heard someone call a famous Colorado mountain Piker's Peak instead of Pike's Peak. Guess who he thought about?"

Shannon sniffed. "Even *I* know better than that. Give a puppy a bad name and she never lives it down."

Juli groaned and corrected, "It's give a *dog* a bad name, not puppy. If you have to quote all those uncool clichés, at least get them right."

"For sure. If you be for tellin' me often enough, who knows what may happen?" Shannon giggled and covered her mouth like a child to keep from waking her friend's parents. "Besides, puppies *are* dogs, aren't they?"

Juli swallowed hard to keep from bawling. Surely nothing too bad could be wrong with Shannon if she could tease like that! Yet after the girls straightened Shannon's messy sheets and she fell into a seemingly untroubled sleep, Juli remained awake. An hour had passed since the other girl's moans first disturbed her. Gray dawn had given way to the promise of another gorgeous spring morning. A choir of birds in the evergreen trees and flowering shrubs that made the Scotts' half-acre lot a thing of beauty, began a morning anthem.

Juli's thoughts ran like a forest fire out of control. Dr. Marlowe had warned it would take a long time for Shannon to regain what the cult had stolen from her. "She came very close to being pushed over the edge," the compassionate doctor quietly told the Scotts and Sean and Grand Riley—Shannon's father and grandfather. "She's going to need counseling, perhaps even deprogramming." Dr. Marlowe drummed her fingers on her desk and looked serious.

"There's a second and even more important concern. In addition to the trauma of being held captive, and starving herself because she knew the food contained drugs, Shannon has to deal with guilt."

"Guilt!" Juli felt anger rise until it threatened to choke

her. "The creeps who took her are to blame, not Shannon. They're the ones who should feel guilty."

"Right, but I doubt they ever will." Dr. Marlowe's quick glance at Juli showed how well she understood the girl's feelings. "Shannon is a Christian, a strong one. What she faces is the knowledge she allowed herself to dabble in the fringe edges of the occult, even though it seemed harmless at the time. Horoscopes, that kind of thing." She raised her hand when Juli started to protest.

"I know someone preyed on her sympathetic nature. Shannon also knows God has long since forgiven anything she may have done that was wrong. Now she has to forgive *herself;* to get beyond the past and on with the future."

Will I ever be as wise as Dr. Marlowe? Juli wondered. *Or Mom and Dad, and Shannon's family? What if I were her? What would I want me, I mean her, to do for me, God? Just love me, I guess, and be there for me.*

Her forehead wrinkled, Juli pondered the questions until an inquisitive ray of spring sunlight poked its nose around the edge of the mini-blinds and danced across the quiet room. It paused at Clue, now sedately sitting on Juli's desk in his usual place. How many hours had he spent watching her do homework and plot stories, waiting for a hug when she felt lonely? The perky red plaid ribbon that came on the box when Clue arrived during the awful year Dad was gone had long since frayed and been replaced. Clue's fur wasn't perfect anymore, either; too much handling. Yet his shiny dark eyes never changed.

The sunbeam lost interest and moved on. For a full minute it rested on Shannon's out-flung hand, but failed to rouse her. Not discouraged, the ray flickered upward and settled on Shannon's wan face.

Juli squeezed her eyes shut and whispered into her pillow. "Lord, please help Shannon get well. Really well, like she was before. She's been through so much. For a while I wondered if our broken friendship would ever heal. Dr. Marlowe says when bones break, once they mend, they're stronger than ever. Please let it be that way with us. Don't let anything ever separate us again."

The peace and comfort of prayer always brought a smile to her lips.

"How come you're grinning like the Cheddar cat?" a sleepy voice demanded from the other bed.

"Not cheddar, Cheshire. Cheddar is cheese!" Juli's laugh rippled out.

Shannon smirked. "So when you get your picture taken, don't they tell you to smile and say cheese?" She hopped out of bed and headed toward the bathroom. "You're impossible!" Juli tossed a pillow in her general direction, but a mocking laugh and closing door left Shannon the victor in their little skirmish.

An hour later, the city bus the girls rode to school noisily stopped by the sidewalk in front of Hillcrest High. Fred Halvorsen, the friendly driver, beamed and went through his usual routine. "Shannon, it's so good to have you back. As I always say, seeing one of you girls without the other—"

"—is like ham without eggs," they chorused. They stepped down from the bus, and Juli's spirits soared. Tall, blond Dave Gilmore and brown-haired Ted Hilton stood waiting for them. Ted spirited Shannon away, leaving Dave to Juli.

"So how's the senior partner of Scott and Gilmore, P.I.s?" he teased. His blue eyes were alight with fun and something a little more that brought a happy feeling to Juli. "AKA—"

"Also known as. . . ," she prompted.

Dave went on as if there had been no interruption. "AKA Julianne; Juli Scott, Super Sleuth; Dave Gilmore's girlfriend *pro tem*—'for the time being,' if you insist on having things spelled out. Did I miss anything?"

"No, but don't call me Julianne," she told him. "Anne's a perfect name for Mom. Hitched on to Juli, it is definitely not cool."

"I've heard worse." He laughed. "Want to know what I've been wondering? What I've been beating my brains trying to decide?"

She forced herself to act casual, and not appear too eager. "Maybe."

Dave grinned again and lowered his voice so the students swarming around them couldn't hear. "What exciting case do you think we'll work on next? Can't you hear the TV news headlines? 'Scott and Gilmore Strike Again.' " He cupped his hands into a make-believe microphone and spoke in a TV news reporter's voice: "Today in an exclusive interview, the highly successful team of Scott and Gilmore modestly disclosed they had recently delivered another shattering blow against crime in the area. Their first two cases pale into insignificance when compared with crime number three. . ." Dave dropped his hands and his voice returned to normal. "Which is?"

Juli couldn't help laughing, but she shook her head and said, "Sorry. If I even smelled a mystery right now, I'd run."

Dave looked skeptical. "I don't think so."

"I mean it." She stopped so suddenly a boy bumped into her, glared, and went on. "I still like mysteries. I still plan to be a mystery writer. I want to have it all, but I'm smart enough to realize I can't have it all at once." She looked deep into his eyes, warmed by the steady look she knew meant real strength. "Right now I'll settle for peace, quiet, and freedom from fear." A lump grew in her throat. "Most of all, I want Shannon to get well."

Dave dropped his teasing and gave her a quick hug. "That's what we all want, Juli. The whole church youth group is praying for her." He took a deep breath and slowly exhaled. "God helped Ted and John and me get Shannon out of that compound. He sure won't let her down now."

"Th–thanks." Juli managed a weak smile. "I just hope it's soon."

Why can't they just leave me alone, Shannon silently shouted after the gazillionth person rushed up to hear all the gruesome details of her experience. *Lord, if one more person asks me what happened, I'll either hit him or her or throw up. The kids back off when Juli or Ted is with me, but I can't have them around holding my hand all the time. It was bad enough when I first came back. I thought it would end soon. But it's worse now. Please, God, make it just go away.*

At her counseling session with Dr. Marlowe later that day, Shannon's misery spilled out. "I just can't handle it," she cried and buried her face in her hands. "I'm a mess. No one but you knows how awful it is. Last night, I mean early this morning, is the first time I've even been able to laugh and talk with Juli the way I used to." A spasm of pain caught her. "Dr. Marlowe, won't it ever be over?"

"Of course." The doctor's no-nonsense voice calmed her a bit. "Shannon, so far you've passively waited for an end to all this to come. It isn't working. You need to fight. It's not going to be easy, but taking action will help you heal."

"I don't know if I can," Shannon confessed. "I feel so drained; it takes all my strength just to get up and off to school." Her fingers nervously picked at her jeans. "Why can't I get my mind off what happened? I even dream about it." Her voice dropped to a whisper. "Dr. Marlowe, I don't have enough energy to be angry."

The physician brought her hands together in a decisive movement. "I'm going to give you an unusual prescription. You're to follow it to the letter. Got it?"

"Got it," Shannon mumbled, wondering if she'd been betrayed. She needed a miracle to stop the fear and nightmares, not a prescription! She silently took the folded note, ran out, and didn't open it until she reached the sidewalk. It said:

Ever hear of the fighting Irish? Be one of them! Satan can't win unless you let it happen. Take a long walk. Listen to the birds sing. Smell the roses. Look at the whitecaps on the bay. Touch a leaf. Shut your mind to everything but God's creation. Then go home and write down every good thing in your life, no matter how small. Bring the list back to me the day after tomorrow.

Shannon couldn't believe her eyes. "No medication? No bed rest? Just take a walk and count my blessings? That's it?" For some reason, it struck her as funny. She stood on the sidewalk and laughed until she cried, never knowing a satisfied Dr. Marlowe watched her through her office window, smiled, and turned away.

Chapter 2

"I smell breakfast." Tall, dark-haired Gary Scott came into the dining room. His stride was slower than his usual ground-covering lope, but laughter set his gray eyes aglow. Their brilliance rivaled the early morning sun shining through the window sun-catchers. "What a day! Makes a man feel like running."

Juli followed her father's glance to the rainbows dancing across the room's pale green walls, then back to the sparkling windows whose wide sill held a multitude of blooming house plants. "Walking, not running," she announced, trying to conceal the obstruction in her throat. Dad's health showed improvement now that he was on leave from his Washington State Patrol job, but he needed a lot more time, just as Shannon did: "Doctor's orders."

Anne Scott, an older edition of Juli, voiced her daughter's unspoken thoughts. "It's so wonderful just to have you home," she exclaimed, the same way she had done every morning since Dad returned. Bright and cheerful-looking in a turquoise pants outfit, she smiled at her family and squeezed each of their hands after Dad asked a blessing on the food.

Juli squeezed back. "What, no red today?" she teased. Anne Scott firmly believed in "down with drab" in clothing, and red was her favorite color.

"The world has enough drab and colorless things without my adding to it," she always said. Practicing what she preached, her morning outfit before going back to teaching the previous fall had been jeans and a scarlet sweatshirt with a "Homemaker First Class" logo.

"My first-graders like turquoise, too," she told Juli.

"And fuchsia. And emerald green. And—"

Dad cut short his daughter's oration by donning a long-suffering look and booming, "And if the females in this family will let the lone, outnumbered male get a word in edgewise, I have an announcement." He laughed and added, "Shannon would probably say *slantwise* instead of *edgewise*."

Juli giggled, more from sheer happiness than at Dad's feeble joke. If ever there were a perfect day, this had to be it. "Even I have to admit Shannon's Rileyisms usually make sense," she defended, tackling her grapefruit.

Mom made a face. "Like when she says, 'Where there's a will, there's a lawyer'? I actually caught myself quoting it that way the other day!"

"Isn't anyone interested in my announcement?" Dad

complained good-naturedly.

"Of course we are." Anne smiled and patted his hand. The happiness in her deep blue eyes made Juli blink. Mom was so much younger-looking and prettier now that Dad's health was improving.

"Okay, what is it?" Juli grinned at Dad and took another bite of grapefruit.

The poker face that had so often baffled wrongdoers couldn't disguise his excitement. "I finished my story."

"You did? Yes!" The clatter of Juli's spoon against her dish when she dropped it was lost in squeals of delight. Every nerve in her body stood at attention. "You actually finished it?"

"I did." Satisfaction oozed from her father. " 'The Black and White Mystery,' alias 'The Case of the Stuffed Skunk,' awaits your slashing red pens, Madame Editors."

Juli rolled her eyes, but couldn't hide her elation. "You aren't really going to call it that, are you?" she asked. Her own dream of one day becoming a mystery writer had helped encourage Dad to try the craft during his convalescence. At first Dr. Marlowe had limited his writing to two hours a day. After a recent checkup, however, she extended the time to four hours, as long as Dad walked at least two miles a day. The schedule worked fine. He worked two hours in the morning and two each afternoon, and still had time to walk and begin dinner for an appreciative wife and daughter.

"Are you satisfied with it, dear?" Anne asked.

Her husband hesitated, then slowly said, "Not exactly satisfied, but realistic enough to know it's the best I can make it at this time."

"That's what you're supposed to do," Juli reminded. "Mrs. Sorenson says if you can't come to that point, you'll worry your story to death."

"Your honors writing teacher should know."

"Should she ever! Now that word's out Mrs. Sorenson is also known as Allison Terrence the author, everyone's trying to get into her classes. Can you imagine ten years and 500 rejection slips before she sold anything? It was worth it, though. Her first novel's receiving great reviews, and she's been contracted to do a series."

Dad grinned. "My one measly story can't compare with that kind of success, but at least it's done. Uh, how soon can you read it?" He sheepishly added, "I just happen to have two extra copies printed out."

He sounded so much like a proud little boy that Anne and Juli exchanged a woman-to-woman look before exclaiming they couldn't wait. "Now's a fine time to tell us," Mom complained. "I can't get to it until my lunch break."

"I can," Juli quickly said. "For once I'm glad Shannon and I ride the bus. Mind if I let her look over my shoulder, Dad?"

"I guess not, if she promises not to steal my idea." Dad smirked. "By the way, remember when I told you I might use the pseudonym 'Juli Scott' for my story? I've changed my mind. You'll have to earn fame and fortune on your own. This is definitely going to be a Gary Scott story. Who knows? It may launch a whole new career for me."

I hope so. I wouldn't have to worry about you going back to police work, and tense up every time you get home late, Juli nearly blurted out. She quickly substituted, "So, where's my copy?"

"And mine?" Anne chimed in.

Dad left long enough to get the copies, then gave a mock sigh. "I suppose they'll come back so marked up it will look like you bled all over them. Oh, well. That's all part of writing." He clasped his hands and pleaded, "Be honest, but please, be kind."

A thread of truth in his stage play struck a sympathetic chord with Juli. How often she yearned for just what Dad had described. Mrs. Sorenson didn't overlook an undotted *i* or an uncrossed *t*. She also crossed out descriptive adjectives in Juli's work and replaced them with strong nouns and vivid verbs.

"I'm sorry you didn't get a chance to enter the magazine contest," Mom said when they walked out the front door together. "Did you tell Shannon you entered her story 'Katie' while she was gone?"

"No. I asked Mrs. Sorenson not to say anything, either." Juli uttered a long, troubled sigh and her voice came out thin. "I don't know why, exactly. Maybe because Shannon's dealing with so much other stuff. Mrs. Sorenson and I both believe 'Katie' deserves to win. If it should, think how surprised Shannon will be."

Understanding lit up Mom's face. "I think you're wise. Shannon doesn't need rejection of any kind right now." Her blue eyes darkened. "How do you think Dad will handle it? Most writers don't sell their first story, do they?"

Juli shook her head and shrugged her shoulders beneath the white t-shirt that topped her denim skirt. "No. Mom, what if Dad's story is really terrible? I'm glad it's done, but almost afraid to read it."

"So am I." She gave Juli an impulsive hug and looked at her watch. "I have to run. See you tonight."

On the bus, Juli and Shannon bent their blond-brown and shining dark heads over "The Black and White Mystery." Juli's gaze raced from sentence to powerful sentence. Shannon gasped, riveted to the pages. Gary Scott had expertly combined his work experience and fascination with mysteries—especially those focused on finding out "who done it," rather than dwelling on gruesome details—to create a spellbinding story.

Pride and relief filled Juli. To think she had doubted. "I never dreamed Dad could write like this!" she burst out. "Do you think I dare ask Mrs. Sorenson to read it?"

Shannon looked troubled. "I don't know. Why don't you just tell her your father wrote a story and let her ask to see it if she wants to? Otherwise, you might be taking advantage of our special friendship with her."

"Good idea. Now, if she will only mention Dad. If she doesn't, I don't know how to bring it up."

Fortune smiled kindly on Juli. After the bell rang for honors writing class, the final class of the day, Mrs. Sorenson asked Juli to stay for a few minutes. "I won't make you miss your bus," she promised.

"No problem. Dave Gilmore is giving me a ride home." Juli felt herself blush at her teacher's keen glance.

"That's nice. He's a fine boy. I asked you to stay because I've learned Shannon's story is under final consideration in the magazine contest. Shall we tell her now? Even if 'Katie' doesn't place, I'm fairly certain a contract will be issued for it at regular magazine rates."

"That is wonderful!" Juli cried. Excitement stirred within her. "She deserves it, Mrs. Sorenson. I can hardly wait for her to find out. But let's wait, okay?"

"That's my feeling, too." Mrs. Sorenson beamed approval and memories stirred in her compassionate eyes. "I remember an 'almost' that left me shattered. By the way, how is your own writing coming?"

"Not so good." Juli shook her head and looked at the floor. Did she dare?

Why not? "I'm the slowpoke in our family. Mom is writing lesson plans and Dad just completed his first short story." There. She'd said it, and without hinting.

"He has!" Interest sparkled in her teacher's eyes. "What did he write?"

"A mystery."

"Why am I not surprised?" Mrs. Sorenson laughed. "What's the title?"

Juli made a face. " 'The Black and White Mystery,' alias 'The Case of the Stuffed Skunk,' believe it or not. I told him it was awful."

"Sounds intriguing. Do you think he'd mind if I read it?"

"Are you sure? I don't want to take advantage of you. I mean, because you're my teacher. I know all kinds of people bother authors, and they don't have much time, and you work all day and have your own writing, and the story is really short, but—"

Mrs. Sorenson smiled. "Stop, please. That is definitely a run-on sentence." When her student automatically flinched, she added, "I really would like to read it. You don't happen to have a copy with you, do you?"

"I thought you'd never ask." Juli's laughter pealed out. Her teacher joined in. Juli handed Mrs. Sorenson her copy. "Thanks a gazillion." *Oh, no! What a dumb thing to say to a writing teacher,* she thought. "Sorry. 'Gazillion is not in the dictionary."

"Expressive, though." Mrs. Sorenson riffled through the pages. "Do you think your father would mind if I edited it for him? I see you have already marked a few places that are a bit awkward."

Juli felt as if someone had given her a signed check with the amount to be determined and filled in by her. "Would you? He'd be thrilled."

"I'll have it back to you tomorrow," the writing teacher promised.

Juli left the room feeling as though she were walking ten feet off the floor.

"Well?" Gary Scott met Juli at the door when she got home. A lock of dark hair dangled over his forehead. Tantalizing aromas from the kitchen bore witness to his culinary efforts.

"Smells good," Juli told him, half-closing her eyes and sniffing like a bloodhound. "Spaghetti?"

"Spanish rice," he impatiently told her. "Where is my story?"

"I don't have it."

Disbelief shot into Dad's gray eyes. "Don't have it! You lost it?"

"No." Juli fought back a smile and said as casually as she could, "Mrs. Sorenson took it home." She ignored her father's rigid pose and open mouth. "She asked if I thought you'd mind if she edited it. I told her you'd be thrilled. Of course, if you'd rather she didn't, I can call her." A laugh bubbled up and spilled over in spite of Juli's best efforts.

Strong arms shot out and seized her shoulders. "Julianne Scott, you gave my story to *Allison Terrence?* She's going to *edit* it?" The shock remained on his face. "I can't believe you asked her to do such a thing!"

Juli laughed harder than ever. "I didn't. We were talking about my writing and it just came up." She repeated the conversation. "It's okay. Mrs. Sorenson really wants to do it. She wouldn't have offered if she didn't." Juli leaned her head on his chest and hugged him. "It's a wonderful story, Dad."

"You're right," a shiny-eyed Anne Scott confirmed from the doorway.

Dad reached out a long arm and welcomed his wife into the circle of love. "I thought it was pretty good," he confessed. "But it's so hard to judge your own work! Are you two sure you aren't prejudiced?"

"Not I," Anne firmly told him.

"Neither am I; Shannon loved it too." Juli couldn't help teasing a little more. "If you don't believe me, just ask her."

Dad didn't have to ask Shannon. She and her father dropped in after dinner. A quiet smile shone on Sean Ryan's face and he shook hands with Dad. "May I see this story my daughter can't stop praising?" the banker asked. "She insisted I come read it."

Gary Scott threw his hands into the air, a gesture of pretended defeat. "A man would think no one ever wrote a story before," he grumbled, but at Sean's insistence he brought out a copy. Juli noticed he also kept an anxious gaze on their friend while Sean read the story.

The banker finished and looked up with a smile. "It's good, Gary. The reason I know is simple. I've never particularly cared for mysteries. . ."—he paused and added significantly—"until now. That should tell you a great deal."

Shannon had the last word in the conversation when

she innocently misquoted, "The real proof of the pudding, as they say, is in the tasting."

"That's in the *eating,*" Juli put in.

"Same thing." Shannon looked wise. "I can hardly wait to hear what Mrs. Sorenson says."

Dad looked so apprehensive that Juli wondered if she had done wrong in passing along the story. The little frown on his face even after the Rileys left increased her discomfort. "Writing's such a private thing," she mumbled instead of doing her homework. "I should have asked Dad's permission. Right, God?" Misery attacked in full force and she hugged Clue. "Lord, when will I learn to stop rushing around doing insensitive things that hurt people? What if Mrs. Sorenson hates the story?" *She can't,* Juli comforted herself. *It's too good.*

CHAPTER 3

The sharp ring of the telephone pierced Juli's misery. Either Dad or Mom picked it up, for no more rings came. A few moments later, Dad called from the living room, "Juli, will you come here?" He sounded strange.

Now what? Juli scrambled off her bed and headed toward the sound of his voice. The peace of the spacious wood-paneled room, drapes closed against the spring darkness, transferred itself to her. She looked at her broadly smiling parents. The call couldn't have been bad news. Every trace of Dad's earlier worry had vanished and Mom looked like she'd just inherited a million dollars.

"You'll never guess who just called." Color flowed into Dad's cheeks. He hugged his daughter, then held her off at arm's length. Before Juli had time to think, he answered his own question. "Would you believe Mrs. Sorenson, AKA Allison Terrence?"

Juli's heart bounced to her throat and lodged there.

"*Mrs. Sorenson* called? How come? I'm not in trouble, am I?" Her forehead puckered. If something were wrong, surely her teacher would have mentioned it after school.

"Guilty conscience?" Dad teased. "Don't worry." He tried to look nonchalant and failed miserably. "She called for two reasons." He ticked them off on his fingers. "First, she warned me she's marking up my manuscript as she does yours."

Juli groaned. Not good news. "And the second reason would be?"

Dad's words rushed out like the Skagit River in flood. "She wanted me to know she's being harsh because she feels it is a very good and probably salable story." A look of awe crept into his face. "She said if it were hers, she would submit it, and keep submitting it until it either sold or she ran out of magazines!"

Juli's knees went weak. She clutched at him for support. "Really?"

"Really. Not bad for a beginner, huh?"

"Not bad at all," she choked out past the excitement in her throat. "Actually, more like *fantastic!* Is it okay for me to call Shannon and her father with the good news?" Her heart thumped out a joyful rhythm. "Mrs. Sorenson tells it like it is. Trust me, I know!"

Gary Scott chuckled and looked more like a proud little boy than ever. "You may stand in the yard and shout it to the whole neighborhood if you like," he told her. But when Juli took a purposeful step toward the front door, he backtracked by adding, "Just kidding. Go call Shannon."

After hearing enough oohs and ahs from Shannon to satisfy even Juli, she came back to the living room and slumped into a chair. "Uh, I know everything turned out okay, Dad, but I owe you an apology. I shouldn't have shown your story without permission. It's just that it was so good, I didn't stop to think." She twisted her fingers. "Sorry."

"Apology accepted." Dad grinned, then grew serious. "You do need to curb your impulses, Juli. You always mean well, but rushing ahead with even the best intentions isn't always wise. Look before you leap is a cliché, but its truth has been proven again and again. Learn to practice it, okay?"

"Okay." Relieved, Juli let a laugh escape. "Shannon said the same thing when I told her how I felt, only she advised me to look before I jumped, not leaped!"

"A true Rileyism, and on that note we need to get to bed," Mom put in. She cocked her head to one side and her sapphire eyes sparkled. "On the other hand, a warm drink might settle us down. Anyone interested?"

"Yes, please," they answered. Dad and Juli followed Mom to the blue and white kitchen with its country-print curtains over mini-blinds. The room's charm and the warm orange-spice herbal tea soon produced yawns. Juli went to bed feeling all was well.

A few blocks away, Shannon Riley and her father also

cradled warm cups in their hands. Their conversation about Gary Scott's good fortune had ended. Shannon looked at her father, silently thanking God for the tall, imposing man whose reserve hid a warm and caring personality. Only their heavenly Father could have been more loving than Sean Riley, especially after the death of beloved wife and mother, Katie, less than two years earlier.

"Dad, do you ever regret leaving Ireland?" Shannon impulsively said.

The dark head so like her own shining, crow-black one moved from side to side without hesitation. "No, *mavourneen,* my little Irish darling. Ireland has too many memories." Two pairs of gray-blue eyes reflected the sadness of those final months in their own country before Sean asked, "Do you?"

"Oh, no. I'd like to go back again someday, though, and take Juli with us."

Sean quietly laughed. Crinkles around his eyes softened the rather severe face that served him well in the banking business. "I can't imagine leaving her behind. As your bus driver friend says, one without the other is—"

Shannon felt the corners of her lips quirk up. "I know . . .like ham without eggs." She turned the cup around and around in her hands. "Dad?"

"What is it, Shannon?"

She took a deep breath. "I–I don't think I'm ready to be back in school." She pressed her lips together hard.

"Every-one keeps asking questions. I get so angry, I want to scream." The cup rattled against her saucer and she quickly set it down. "Could you take some time off, even a few days?"

"I can and I will—as much as you need." His strong hand covered hers.

Thank God for her father's decisiveness! The tension in Shannon's shoulders fled like morning mist over Bellingham Bay when chased by a strong wind.

"Do you want to go away? Not to Ireland, of course." His eyes twinkled.

She closed her eyes. A succession of pictures ran through her mind. A peaceful white colonial-style mansion, complete with tall columns and set atop a high bluff. Deer, rabbits, squirrels, and a multitude of birds, all protected by No HUNTING signs. Rustling cottonwood leaves and shivering birch trees, whispering secrets along the banks of a sweeping river. A forest in the background. White-haired Ryan Riley, called Grand by family and friends.

"Dad," Shannon whispered. "Take me to the Skagit House."

"We'll go tomorrow morning," he promised. "As soon as I can arrange time off from the bank."

"We need to pick up my school assignments, too," Shannon reminded, mentally already halfway to her grandfather's inn on the road between Rockport and Darrington, southeast of Bellingham.

"That's no problem," Sean quietly said. He stood, came to where she sat, and dropped a loving hand on her shoulder, following it with a light kiss on her forehead. "Your principal, Mr. Smiles, I believe you call him, told me earlier that if you needed extra time, everything can be arranged."

Shannon blinked back tears at the round-faced principal's kindness. Ever since her rescue from the Children of Light compound, she cried easily, especially when people were good to her. Dr. Marlowe said the tears were so close to the surface because Shannon had held them back too long, and that it was okay and necessary to cry. Maybe time at the Skagit House would help her get control of her emotions. *I hope so, God,* she silently prayed. *I'm beginning to feel like a waterfall.*

The ridiculous thought made her feel better. She fell asleep in a surprisingly short time after her head hit the pillow. No nightmares tonight, but a dream of the Skagit House and the peace it offered.

At breakfast the next morning, Sean suggested they invite Juli and her parents to the inn for the weekend. "Some of your other friends, too," he offered. "I talked to Grand on the phone and he doesn't have a lot of reservations. There's enough room for the Scotts and two others." He raised a knowing eyebrow. "I suspect it will be Ted Hilton and Dave Gilmore."

"Bingo!" Shannon felt a warm blush coloring her cheeks. Of all the boys at school or church, none rated higher with her than brown-haired Ted Hilton. His laughing blue eyes, patience, and loyal devotion to his shallow, bottle-blond twin sister Amy made Shannon's heart beat faster. Juli felt the same way about Dave. Not mushy; just happy to be together, spiced with deep friendship.

The Rileys' plans ran into a snag when Shannon called Juli from her bedroom phone. Not about the weekend, but about Shannon leaving that day. "You can't," Juli flatly told her. "Don't you know what day this is?"

"Wednesday. So what?" Shannon frowned at the phone.

"So our youth group is having a meeting right after school to decide if we want to do the Adopt-a-Grandparent visiting program for older people, especially shut-ins. We're giving the report, remember?"

"I–I guess I forgot." She took a deep breath. "Do you really need me?"

"Like cheeseburgers need cheese. Can't you wait and go tomorrow? One day won't make all that much difference, will it?"

The Irish girl thought of how peaceful it would be at Skagit House, and reluctantly said, "I guess not. I just need some space."

"Your house is quiet. Stay home from school and rest," Juli suggested. "Oh, we're going to the Pizza Palace afterward. Can you really turn down mozzarella, pepperoni, and all the other good stuff?"

Shannon felt herself weakening. "Fat chance. Hold on, will you?" She covered the mouthpiece and called out to her father, "I forgot Juli and I have to make a report to the youth group. Okay to wait until tomorrow? I'll stay home today."

Sean came to the doorway, knotting a tie between the points of a crisp shirt collar. "Better, actually. It will give me time to clear my desk. See you tonight." He smiled and disappeared.

"It's okay," Shannon said into the phone. "Someone has to pick me up, though."

"We will," Juli said. "I have to run. See you."

Shannon hung up, thinking of the blue Honda Accord she'd had such a short time. Her father sold it immediately after the police found it abandoned by her captors. Shannon couldn't look at it without remembering the day she'd been abducted. Sean promised to get her another car when she felt ready to help choose it. So far Shannon had put it off, unwilling to face making any more choices than she absolutely had to.

Alone in the small, two-story brick home with its many-paned windows and carved front door, Shannon curled up on the couch and flipped on the TV. She fell asleep during a boring movie, then padded to the kitchen for a sandwich and milk when she awakened. Forcing herself to eat every bite, she yawned, stumbled upstairs to her room, and fell asleep again.

"Thanks, God," she murmured when she awoke a second time. Her voice sounded loud in the quiet room. "Three o'clock! Mercy me, how I slept." She stretched, yawned, and felt better than she had for a long time. A quick call alerted Dr. Marlowe to the fact that her patient would be out of town for several days. By the time Dave Gilmore's blue '68 Mustang pulled up out front, Shannon had showered and climbed into black jeans and a bright red knit shirt.

Juli, eyes looking bluer than ever above her light blue top and white jeans, hopped from the passenger seat so Shannon could climb in back with Ted Hilton. Shannon didn't mind the close quarters. Being with her best friends wrapped her in a blanket of security and happiness. Hope burned brightly. Soon she'd be able to put the past behind her, as Dr. Marlowe promised. *The sooner, the greater,* she prayed, never knowing she'd misquoted again, this time to God!

Shannon and Juli presented their reports with such enthusiasm, the entire youth group voted to accept the Adopt-a-Grandparent program. The only dissenting vote came from Amy Hilton. She smoothed her pink t-shirt and flowered skirt and complained, "I don't know when I'll have time. I barely get around to visiting my own grandmother, let alone someone else's." Her light blue eyes showed annoyance. "It might not be so bad if we could work in teams." She turned wistful eyes toward Dave Gilmore, who just grinned.

Shannon and Juli exchanged one of their perfect-communication-without-saying-a-word looks. It said: *Leave it to Amy to try and turn a youth group project into a man-*

hunt! Too bad. She would be a lot prettier if she'd leave off the heavy makeup and pouty expression. She can be nice when she stops trying to be Miss Popularity. Poor Ted, to have to put up with a twin like her!

Today Amy had a new grievance. Someone had grazed the secondhand red Mustang convertible she bought with money inherited from an aunt. The car was in a shop being repaired. "They've had it for ages," she moaned.

Who cares? Juli wordlessly communicated to Shannon, who turned away to hide a laugh.

"Who's for the Pizza Palace?" Ted asked.

It turned out several members of the group couldn't go. Only Shannon and Juli, the Hiltons, Dave, John Foster and his new girlfriend Molly Bowen, were free.

"I'll have to go with you," Amy told her brother, after glancing toward John's VW Bug. Her sulky face showed how much being without a date bothered her.

Ted and Shannon were already in the back seat. "No way," Ted said bluntly. "There's no room, and this car only has four seat belts."

Amy turned sullen. "Then I'll go home." The corners of her mouth drooped.

"You can go with John and me," a soft voice invited. Redheaded Molly's warm brown eyes held nothing but welcome. The freckles Ted insisted on calling speckles dotted her nose and clear, pink cheeks.

Amy hesitated. "I get carsick if I sit in the back seat." She looked up at John through mascara-coated lashes.

"I don't mind sitting in back." Molly smiled at John, whose thundercloud face showed a struggle between courtesy and disgust. She clambered in. "Come on, Amy. See you all at the Pizza Palace!"

"Yeah." Dave tore his gaze from the retreating VW and held the door for Juli. "Some girl, huh."

"Yeah." Shannon leaned forward and nudged Juli's shoulder in an effort to switch her friend from boiling to simmer. "Great afternoon. Those puffy white clouds look too lazy to move."

"All this and pizza, too," Dave commented, attending to his driving. He suddenly laughed. "This wonderful Wednesday's pretty nice after our mysterious Monday and troublesome Tuesday."

Shannon wholeheartedly agreed. "This is my cup of chocolate."

"If it weren't a wonderful Wednesday, I'd tell you it's tea, not chocolate," Juli teased. "Since it is, you can tell Dave and Ted about this weekend."

"Gladly." Shannon turned to Ted and felt herself blush. The unguarded look in his eyes certainly made a girl feel special.

CHAPTER 4

The Pizza Palace occupied part of a large lot and shared paved parking with the Chuckanut Community Bank. Evergreen trees and a wealth of blooming flowers, not to mention terrific food, drew customers like a beach draws sun-lovers, especially teens. Parents heartily approved of the spotlessly clean, no-smoking atmosphere and the fact that the strongest drink they served was root beer.

Dave swung the Mustang into the lot and expertly parked close beside John Foster's VW. "It's going to take a while. Look at the cars."

Juli licked her lips in anticipation. "It'll be worth waiting for."

"Right. If someone held a Pizza of the Year contest, the Pizza Palace would win hands up," Shannon added.

"You mean hands down," Ted corrected.

Shannon shook her dark head. "No, I don't. Once I get my hands on the pizza, they're going straight up to my mouth!"

The others groaned as they all got out of the car.

"I wonder why Amy's sounding off," Juli whispered to Dave, keeping her voice low so Ted couldn't hear her.

It wouldn't have mattered. Ted marched straight to his sister and demanded, "What are you babbling about now?"

"Look." Amy pointed to a beautifully restored classic white Mustang.

"So? You've seen Mustangs before." Ted grinned and mischief danced in his blue eyes. "You even own one, remember?"

She spun toward him, eyes throwing sparks. "Of course, but this one reminds me it's going to be practically forever before I can drive my convertible again, just because some stupid person—"

"Stop griping. I'm hungry." He grabbed his protesting sister by the shoulder and marched her toward the door.

"I'm cold," she complained, crossing her arms. "Where's your letter jacket?"

"In the car, right where it's going to stay. Move it, will you?"

"No. I'm cold." Amy obstinately refused to take another step. "You'd think my own twin brother would care if I get pneumonia."

Ted muttered something under his breath, but released her. "On a day like this? Oh, all right. Unlock the door, will you, Dave?"

Three minutes later the group joined their laughing companions waiting inside. They argued good-naturedly over what they wanted on their pizzas, then snagged a table big enough for all seven of them. Amy looked ridiculous in Ted's sapphire blue jacket with its large white "Pirates" emblem blazoned on the back. Getting her own way hadn't improved her attitude, either. She flirted with Dave and John, then scowled even more when neither of them acted interested.

Juli noticed the cheerleader's bad mood didn't stop her from eating an incredible amount of pizza when it finally came. It never ceased to amaze Amy's acquaintances just how much food she could stuff into her tiny body.

"Anyone mind if I have the last piece?" Amy turned on the charm and reached for it. Just before it got to her mouth, someone trying to get between the closely spaced tables lurched into Amy's chair. The impact jolted the slice of pizza from her hand, straight onto Ted's treasured letter jacket.

"Hey, watch where you're going!" Ted exclaimed.

"Sorry." The offender moved on.

Ted stared at his mutilated jacket. "Thanks a lot, Amy."

"It's not my fault some guy bumped into me," she shrilled. "I hope it didn't get on my skirt." She anxiously peered down and groaned when she saw the mess.

The other girls were already busy dipping napkins into water glasses and trying to mop up the spill as best they could. "Better take the jacket straight to the cleaners," Juli advised. "Your skirt's washable, isn't it, Amy?"

"Yes, but tomato stains are tough to get out," the angry

girl said sullenly. She brushed off an offending piece of pepperoni. "I knew I shouldn't have come."

Juli intercepted a *too-bad-you-did* look from Shannon. Despite all their attempts to like Amy, scenes like this made it difficult. Juli once confessed to her friend, "I'm glad God says to love everyone, not like them. It's a lot easier!"

Now she asked, "What do we owe?" Because the group spent so much time together, they had a standing rule of "pay and pay alike," as Shannon said, unless it was a specific date. It took several minutes to reach the cashier and settle their bill. Dave had just started to open the door for the others when a siren wailed. The sound grew to a scream, drowning out the laughter and clink of glasses inside the Pizza Palace.

"Wonder what's happening? Sure sounds close." Dave jerked the door open. He and his friends spilled out, along with the rest of the customers and most of the staff. At the same moment, two police cars with lights flashing, closely followed by two more, tore into the parking lot and screeched to a stop in front of the Chuckanut Community Bank. Uniformed officers burst from the cars and into the bank.

"Uh-oh. Looks like a robbery." Dave sounded as excited as Juli felt.

Ted whipped toward Shannon, whose face had turned paper white. "There's nothing to be afraid of," he told her, dropping a comforting arm over her shoulders. "It must be all over or the officers wouldn't go barging in like that.

They'd approach with a whole lot more caution."

Color gradually came back to her face. "I–I'm all right." Yet her stunned look betrayed the fact Shannon still had a long way to go before again becoming the girl her friends used to know.

When it became obvious no danger existed, Dave and Juli, and Molly and John walked across the parking lot toward the bank and a police officer who had emerged and gone back to the patrol car. Amy refused to budge. Ted and Shannon also hung back from the crowd of curious on-lookers.

"Stay back," the officer ordered, a disgusted look on her face. "Excitement's over. He got away, just like before."

Just like before? Juli didn't remember hearing Chuckanut Community Bank had been robbed. She turned to Dave. His eyes held two question marks. They sent a shiver through Juli. So did his low comment, "And to think it happened on Wonderful Wednesday. At least we aren't involved."

"Right." Relief surged through Juli. "As I said before, no mysteries are good mysteries right now."

"That's not quite a Rileyism, but close," Dave teased. When she didn't reply, he prodded, "Didn't you hear me?"

Juli stuck her nose in the air and smirked. "I'm not hard of hearing; I'm ignoring you. Okay?"

He ruffled her blondish-brown hair with one hand and had the last word. "Okay, but just remember: It's a long walk from here to the Scott and Riley residences for girls who don't show the driver enough respect."

They reached Dave's Mustang and climbed inside. "I suppose this will be on the evening news," Shannon said on the way home. She still looked a little pale.

"All the details plus a lot of speculation," Ted predicted. The corners of his mouth tilted into a lopsided grin. "It will be interesting to hear all the reporters' theories. Wonder if they will vaguely resemble what really happened."

Shannon put in, "Just think. We were right on the crime scene."

"Close." Juli giggled. It felt good to hear Shannon sounding more natural. "The quote is really 'on the scene of the crime,' but in this case, your version fits better."

"Good going, Shannon." Ted's irrepressible sense of humor shifted into high. "Pretty soon you'll have us all tossing Rileyisms around like basketballs."

"Don't hold your breath," Juli warned. She abruptly changed the subject. "I can't wait to get to the Skagit House this weekend. Dad and Mom are excited, too. It's been a while."

"Too long," Shannon fervently agreed.

Something in her friend's voice prevented Juli from saying more. So did the longing in the gray-blue Irish eyes. *Please, God,* Juli prayed, *help her find peace. I miss the real Shannon so much.*

That night the TV news reports proved sketchy. All contained the basic facts. A male figure had come into the

Chuckanut Community Bank, ski cap pulled low, denim jacket collar turned up. They effectively hid the robber's face. He approached a teller, pulled a gun, and gave the woman a note that read, "Hand over the bills in your cash drawer. Keep your mouth shut until I'm gone. No one goes near the windows or comes out for at least ten minutes. If not—" A crude drawing of a skull and crossbones served as a signature.

The teller kept her head and obeyed orders to the letter. She forced herself to remain calm, as she'd been trained to do if a situation like this should ever occur.

The robber, who could have been anyone, simply walked out with several hundred dollars and vanished. No one had seen anything out of the ordinary. And no one except the teller even knew a crime had been committed until it was all over.

According to the news, investigators were saying nothing about suspects or possible clues, other than mentioning that a similar holdup had taken place across town a few weeks earlier. Officials refused to comment about whether the two incidents might be related, but not the TV anchor persons. They more than made up for the official silence by speculating about the possibility of a pattern.

Both bank officials and police officers openly praised the teller's refusal to try and be a heroine. "This woman *is* a heroine," one reporter insisted. "Her own life and the lives of several others were threatened. A single shout could well have made the difference between robbery and a shooting, perhaps even death. She is to be congratulated."

"What chance is there he will be caught?" Juli asked her father when the newscast ended.

Gary Scott grinned at his daughter. "Do you want a police officer's answer or a mystery writer's answer?" he teased.

She threw the ball back to his court. "Either."

"I could write a dozen clues that would lead to the capture of the bank robber," he told her smugly. A moment later, he became serious. "Solving crimes in real life is a whole different story, though, and I don't mean that as a pun."

"You're right about that." Juli sighed. "I'd better go do my homework." She headed for her room. Once there, she found it hard to concentrate. She finally gave up, dropped to her bed, and stared at Clue. His shiny dark eyes faithfully stared back, but they didn't stop the whirlpool of thoughts circling in her brain. Maybe writing in her journal would help. She took the notebook Mom had given her all those months before, flipped through it, and read snatches here and there. Then she picked up her pen and began writing.

> *Why do people do bad things, God—like robbing banks? Was the man today high on drugs? It's so stupid! He must have known he wouldn't walk away with a whole lot of money. Everyone knows tellers don't keep huge amounts in their tills. He*

also must have known he might not walk away at all. Dumb. Even if he doesn't believe in You, why would he risk a long prison sentence for armed robbery?

The worst thing about people choosing to do wrong is how much it hurts others. Look how many innocent people die because other people, including a whole lot of kids my age, drink and cause terrible accidents. Girls and women abuse their bodies with alcohol and drugs, and then their newborn babies have to go through with-drawal. God, it just isn't fair!

Angry tears blurred Juli's vision. How could anyone who knew she was going to be a mother do that to her unborn child? The upset girl reached for a tissue, wiped her eyes, and picked up her pen again.

Today, when Shannon saw those police cars, she looked like she was going to faint. It must have brought back all her horrible memories. I'm glad she's going to Skagit House. I'm glad she will have a couple of days just with her dad and Grand before the rest of us get there.

Juli nibbled the end of her pen, then slowly added,

It's a good thing You're in charge of the world,

Lord, and not me. I don't think I could stand
back and let people choose sin if I had the power
to keep them from doing it. I'd probably make
everyone be good. I know You give all of us the
right to choose. It's just that this would be such a
great world if everyone chose You.

If it hadn't been for You, Mom and I would
never have made it through Dad being gone, and
he wouldn't be home now. Thanks for always
being there for us, God. I know You'll get
Shannon through this, too, but please, could You
hurry?

Juli reread the last sentence and started to cross out the last five words. She stubbornly shook her head. "No," she whispered to Clue. "God won't be offended. He *wants* me to let Him know how I feel." She hugged her squishy, cinnamon-brown bear friend, put her journal away, and reached for her homework.

Much as she liked school, the next two days at Hillcrest High dragged. Juli's feet carried her through the halls and to the cafeteria. Her body sat in her usual place. She answered when called on in class. Yet her thoughts continually strayed to Shannon, the Skagit House, and the upcoming weekend.

"Come back, come back, wherever you are. . . ." Dave Gilmore chanted as he walked her from the bus to the school building Friday morning.

"Okay." Juli gave a happy little skip. "I just can't wait until school's out so we can head for the Skagit House. Too bad Shannon and her Dad took the van. It has room for all of us to go together."

Dave regretfully shook his blond head. "Ted and I couldn't go with you anyway. Dad and Mom already had plans for tonight. They're picky about who babysits Christy, so I'm it." He hastily added, "I don't blame them. If I had an eight-year-old kid, I wouldn't want just anyone taking care of her." He caught Juli's hand and swung it. "Ted and I will be up early tomorrow morning."

A burst of happiness made Juli taunt, "In time for breakfast, I'm sure."

"*Second* breakfast," Dave corrected. "Ted and I don't mind starting out when the roosters crow, but on an empty stomach? No way." He tilted his head and grinned maddeningly. "We're growing boys, remember?"

"You'll be groaning boys if you eat two breakfasts," Juli warned.

"We'll risk it. The food at Skagit House is to die for!" He smacked his lips.

Why should the familiar expression start chills up and down Juli's spine?

CHAPTER 5

Shannon Riley enjoyed every mile of the long drive from Bellingham to the Skagit House. Between school, church, friends, and her father's demanding duties at the bank, they didn't have a lot of time to just talk.

"It's certainly a best-of-Bellingham day, isn't it?" Sean observed. His casual pants, open-necked shirt, and running shoes contrasted sharply with the business suit he usually wore at this time of day.

Shannon peered through the window and gave a little bounce of happiness, taking care not to release her seat belt. "Is it ever! Last night's rain makes the world look like it just had its face washed."

Her father laughed. "You do have a way with words, my own colleen."

"That's what Mrs. Sorenson says, except the colleen part." Shannon rubbed a frown from her forehead. "I thought she'd say something about my story 'Katie' not getting entered in the contest, but she hasn't."

Sean gave his daughter a quick look and blandly said, "I imagine Juli talked with your teacher and explained."

Some of the day's joy drained from Shannon. "I missed out on a lot because of what happened, didn't I?" She saw his hands tighten on the wheel before he silently nodded. "Dad, I still can't believe I was dumb enough to get mixed up with those people, even though they seemed sincere." Her words became heavy with emotion as she added, "I caused so much trouble and worry to you and Grand and my friends."

"Thank God, it's over," he huskily said. "You have learned an important lesson, *mavourneen.* Satan knows no one would follow him if he appeared as he really is—slimy and evil. Instead, he plants the desire for power and control in people's hearts, then sits back laughing and watches his seeds grow." Sean's right hand slipped from the wheel long enough to give Shannon's arm a loving pat.

"I'm proud of the progress you're making, even though I know how hard it is." He expertly changed lanes to avoid traffic merging onto I-5.

"For both of us," she added, taking a deep breath.

"Yes." He shot her a quick glance and smiled. "We're in this together, you know." To her surprise, he laughed.

"What's funny?" She sat up straighter and stared at him. Her father was one good-looking man, especially when laughter brightened his rather serious countenance. *No wonder Mother fell in love with him!* Sean Riley needed no blarney to be attractive. Shannon's blue-gray eyes, so like his, opened wide. Did other women find him appealing? They must. How could they help it?

"Dad, are you going to get married again? Someday, I mean." She blurted it out, then covered her mouth with one hand and scrunched down in the seat.

"I don't know. It will depend on a great many things." Her father's usual reserve raised an invisible wall between them.

Suddenly it seemed the most important thing on earth to know. Shannon crashed through the unseen barrier. "Meaning me?"

"Of course." A smile warmed Sean's face. "How would you feel about it?"

"I don't know," she answered. How *would* she feel?

"Nothing must ever come between us, Shannon. Right now, you're all I need. On the other hand, in a few years you'll be through college and married."

Her heart beat faster with sympathy. "And you'll be alone."

"I'm afraid so. Your mother and I had a wonderful marriage. No woman on earth can or will ever take her place." Shannon knew he spoke from the depths of his heart, something her father didn't often do, even with her. "If I'm to remarry—and I know your mother would want me to do so if it might bring happiness—it will be an additional love, not a replacement. I'm content to leave the future in the hands of God." His eyes twinkled. "For your information, I'm not out shopping for a wife!"

"Good." Shannon thought of her feelings for Ted Hilton, the joy that came from simply being with him, the exciting possibility that maybe someday. . . She rested her hand on her dad's knee so she wouldn't interfere with his driving. "I'd hate to think of you going through long, lonely years," she whispered, so low he had to bend his fine head to hear her. "If God sends the right woman, I think I can be happy for you. That's half the fight, right?"

"Half the *battle,* but I certainly hope it doesn't come to that!" Sean chuckled.

It brought an answering smile and steadied Shannon's trembling lips. She dropped into brogue. "I'm glad there'll be no weddin' soon. Your one and only daughter's for needin' her father right now." She scooted as close as her seat belt allowed, and pressed her shining dark head against his shoulder for a moment, then determinedly broke the mood. "Remember when I was a wee child? I always asked how many hours 'twould be before we got where we were going."

"I certainly do!" Sean chuckled again. A flood of warm memories poured into the van as father and daughter relived their life in Ireland. Their do-you-remembers shortened the miles, and long before noon, they reached the Skagit House. Shannon anxiously surveyed it to make sure nothing had changed. She gave a sigh of relief when Grand hurried from the open front door and reached the van the moment it stopped. Had anyone ever possessed whiter hair, keener eyes, more welcoming arms? She flew into them. "Seen any leprechauns lately?" she demanded.

"Don't be mockin' the little folk," Ryan Riley scolded. He sent a look of pretend alarm toward the gorgeous background of birch and alder, hemlock and fir, pine and cedar behind the mansion-style inn. That's where he always teasingly insisted leprechauns lived and frolicked in the moonlight when self-respecting mortals slept the best part of the night away.

She hugged him, hard. "It's so good to be here." A few minutes later, she repeated the words in the privacy of her bedroom. Located on the northeast corner of the second floor, two large canopied beds and faded lavender brocaded walls gave a long-ago feel to the room she loved. The enormous walk-in closet and adjoining bathroom added more modern conveniences. Shining casement windows, curtained in pale green with tiny lavender flowers, overlooked the back of the property. Shannon had heard thousands of bird songs from outside those windows. She had seen hundreds of wild animals, including deer and occasionally a coyote. She had also watched rain and snow beat against them, shutting her in a cozy, secure place.

Now she opened the windows, leaned out, and breathed deeply. No pollution here, just the perfume of roses in full bloom and the tang of freshly mown grass. They brought peace and a wave of exhaustion. Shannon yawned, stumbled to the nearest bed, and threw back the spread that matched the curtains. The familiar mattress welcomed her.

Less than a minute after her head hit the pillow, she fell into a deep and untroubled sleep. It brought more healing than all the medicine in Dr. Marlowe's cabinets.

That afternoon and all day Friday, Shannon found herself content to "play lady, lazy, or all of the above," as she put it. She ate the excellent meals the staff served. She adopted the Mexican siesta habit and slept each afternoon, as well as nights. She wandered the grounds alone or with Sean, and spent time propped against a tree on the bluff overlooking the Skagit River, just thinking.

Sean had given Shannon a magazine article about a girl just a little older than she who had been through a similar ordeal. "Even though it brings back bad memories, I believe it will help you," he said. "Especially the last paragraph."

Shannon took the article to her favorite perch above the slow-moving, shadowed river. She felt cold sweat crawl up her spine when she read how the girl writing the story was kidnapped from her own home and held prisoner. A half dozen times the Irish girl put the article down. Yet its fascination forced her to pick it up and go on. She came to the closing paragraph, written in the victim's own words:

"My kidnapper stole part of my life. Nothing I can do will get it back. Now I have a choice: I can leave what happened behind me. If I don't, the kidnapper will still be in control, even though I'm free and he's in prison. I know it won't be easy, but with the help of God, I'm going to do whatever it takes to move on. I refuse to let some creep steal any more of my life!"

"Good for you!" Shannon cried.

An eagle wheeling in the clear spring sky dipped a wing, as if agreeing with the solitary figure far below. The river murmured a song of approval. Thankfulness filled Shannon's heart. She bowed her head and closed her eyes. Words did not come, but she knew her Father in heaven heard the silent cries of her soul. A long time later she whispered, "Whatever it takes, God."

That night at dinner, she told her father, Grand, and the Scotts how much the story of the courageous girl had helped her. She saw the glad look that sprang to their faces. It made her more determined than ever to get on with her life.

"Makes a lot of sense," Gary Scott told her. "I've been fighting the same kind of thing." He looked thoughtful. "One thing that helped me a lot was returning to the spot where my nightmare all began. Have you thought about going back to the compound near Mount Baker?"

Shannon instantly felt sick. She pushed back from the table and tried to stand. Her knees played traitor and refused to hold her. She slid back down to the chair.

"I'm sorry I mentioned it. It's obviously too soon." Gary's voice cut through the dizziness and roaring in Shannon's ears. She closed her eyes and shook her head to clear it.

"It's okay. I–I just. . ." *Please God, give me strength,* she silently prayed. A feeling she was not alone helped her reopen her eyes. The circle of concerned faces reassured her.

"We don't want you to do anything until you're ready," Sean said.

"I have to," she cried through stiff lips. "If I wait until I'm ready, it will be the thirteenth of never."

Juli shoved a hand over her mouth and ducked her head.

Even in her turmoil, Shannon knew it was to keep from laughing. "What?"

"It's the twelfth of never, but who cares?" Juli fiercely demanded. She got up so fast her chair slid back, and hugged her friend hard. "Do you really mean it? Are you willing to go back to the compound?"

"No, but I'm going, if Dr. Marlowe says I can. Why should I be afraid of a deserted camp in the woods?" *Had her grim voice spoken those words,* Shannon wondered?

"You shouldn't be afraid, especially when you'll have Dave and Ted and me right there to protect you," Juli promised. Her blue eyes darkened. "You do want us to go, don't you? I mean, it's okay if you'd rather have your father, but, but—good grief, I'm blathering on, as you call it, aren't I?"

"You are, but I do want you to go. Okay, Dad?" Shannon sent an anxious look toward her parent. Would he understand that having Juli and some of her rescuers along would make it easier?

Anne Scott joined the conversation. "I'd feel a whole

lot better it we all went." Shannon glanced at her in surprise, but Juli's mother continued. "I'm sure no one's hanging around the compound. On the other hand, the unoccupied buildings could look mighty inviting to someone looking for a hiding place."

"You're becoming as suspicious as your husband and daughter," Sean teased. "I have to agree with you, though. What about next Saturday? Grand, you'll go too?"

"I think I'll be for leavin' the mysteries to you young folks," Grand said. "Besides, near as we can tell, there's nothin' to see but deserted buildings."

Shannon shivered. "I hope that's all."

"I don't." Attention swung to Juli, who stuck her chin in the air. "I wish we'd find the cult leaders right there waiting for Dad to come arrest them."

"Fat chance," Shannon muttered.

Then Gary Scott exclaimed, "Hold it! I'm an author, not an officer, remember?"

Juli's eyes flashed. "An officer on leave," she stubbornly reminded. "With the power to arrest criminals."

"Your imagination is running away with you," her mother told her. "We'll find an empty camp, let Shannon have the time she needs there, and have a picnic on the way home. Okay?"

"Double okay," Shannon answered. She sent Mom a grateful smile, thinking, *If God wants Dad to remarry, I hope his new wife will be like my second mom.* The band of dread around Shannon's heart loosened. Yet all weekend long, every time anyone mentioned the following Saturday's plans, a squiggly little feeling of fear made her shiver. The only thing that could make it go away was repeating the words that had become a slogan, "I'll do whatever it takes."

"Dad?" she asked Sunday afternoon when the boys, Juli and her parents, and Sean Riley prepared to go back to Bellingham. "Is it all right if I stay here a few more days? I have all my lessons, so I won't get behind. It's kind of lonesome in Bellingham with you working." She glanced down at her tightly twisted fingers. "After next Saturday, I should be able to go back to school."

Sean's clear eyes looked deep into her troubled ones. "Do you want me to stay? I can call the bank and tell them I need more time."

She thought it over. "I think I'd rather have you save your vacation days so we can go somewhere this summer. I'll be fine here, and Grand says he will bring me in Friday afternoon."

"That I will," the kindly old man agreed. "A body needs time with his granddaughter, and she's the grrrrandest of them all, I'm for thinkin'."

"I have to agree on that." Sean laughed. "All right. See you Friday." He hugged Shannon. "Don't worry about next weekend. We'll all be there for you. God will, too, you know.

She blinked drops from her lashes. "I know. I couldn't do it otherwise."

Six happy days later, with Dr. Marlowe's hearty approval, the Scotts, Rileys, Dave, and Ted buckled themselves into Sean's van. A full picnic basket contributed to a festive air, and mouthwatering aromas made the boys plead for samples. Juli sternly denied their request with, "Remember what I said about groaning, boys. Not a taste."

Shannon joined in the laughter. She innocently added to it by remarking, "The little towns are sure far and few between, aren't they?" When Juli told her she meant few and far between, Shannon just grinned. But all the fun in the world couldn't remove the icy lump of fear that had formed in the pit of her stomach and grew larger and colder with every passing mile.

CHAPTER 6

Protected by family and friends, Shannon stepped from the van. Her heart pounded until she felt she would suffocate. She stared at the gate in the high chain-link fence surrounding the compound, located deep in the forest where she had been held prisoner. The padlock had disappeared. The gate creaked with a protesting screech at Gary Scott's touch.

Shannon took a deep breath and walked inside, closely followed by the others. She stared at the empty compound. "It's the same, only different," she mumbled.

"Is it ever!" Dave Gilmore agreed. "No chanting and ranting. No stink of marijuana smoke. Just empty buildings."

Shannon stared. Her heartbeat returned to normal. "This isn't as bad as I thought it would be," she announced.

"That's because you weren't ever actually in the main buildings," Sean said. He put his arm around her.

"That's right. I was drugged and woke up in the cabin. The only time I was out of it was once when I sneaked to the gate and found it locked."

"You were also out of it when we rescued you," Ted reminded her, his face grim.

Shannon turned toward a small log cabin a little distance from the other buildings. Her mouth became dry. "I-I have to go in there." She pointed.

"All right." Her father's arm tightened on her shoulders and Juli crowded close on the other side.

"We're right here," she said in a choky voice. She grabbed Shannon's hand and squeezed it hard.

This is it, Shannon thought when they reached the cabin. *Lord, please be with me.* Instantly the words from the 23rd Psalm she had clung to in her trial returned to strengthen her: "I will fear no evil, for thou art with me," she whispered.

She stepped inside. The cabin also was the same yet different. Bright sunlight and bird songs drifted through the open window. The curtain blew just as before. The same woodsy smell tickled her nose. The rough board walls were the same, as was the hard cot on which she had tossed, turned, and tried to sleep. She gazed around the primitive cabin. Not a scrap of clothing hung on the wall hooks. The rude table and chair looked barren and lonely. Mouse droppings in a corner and the chewed remainder of a deserted bread sack showed no one had occupied the hut since Shannon left, except for wild creatures.

A rush of relief poured through her. "I'm not afraid," she exclaimed. "There's nothing here to frighten me. It's almost too true to be good!"

Juli giggled. "You mean 'too good to be true,' but aren't you glad it isn't?"

Shannon freed herself from Sean's arm and whirled around the empty room, gloriously happy, wonderfully free. "I may misquote things, but at least I make sense," she jeered. "I feel like I could dance all day."

"Dance all *night,* dance all night!" Julie shouted, but a burst of laughter from the rest of the group drowned her out.

Ted Hilton looked thoughtful and suggestively rubbed his middle. "Now that Shannon and Company have slain her dragon of fear, how about some food? I'm starving." He pretended to collapse against Shannon, to the others' amusement.

"We didn't kill the dragon; God did," she soberly reminded. "Thanks, everyone." She blinked hard and found herself ravenous. "I'm almost as hungry as Ted. Let's go." She marched out of the cabin, feeling ten feet tall. "I know it isn't realistic, but right now I feel as if nothing can ever hurt any of us again."

"I hope she's right, even though it puts Scott and Gilmore, P.I.'s, out of business," Dave whispered to Juli. "Right, Super Sleuth?"

"We can always work on mysteries that involve other people," she whispered back, too happy just then to care if she never heard of another mystery. "What odds do I get that Shannon will be back in school Monday?"

"Are you kidding? None! I'd say it's a sure thing." Dave beamed. His blue eyes showed he shared Juli's joy. So did the quick hug he gave her before they followed Shannon and Company across the compound to the van.

Several miles down the road they found a roadside park next to a merry little stream. The enormous lunch Mom and Juli had packed vanished before the onslaught of hungry people. They also took time to enjoy the cool shade under the trees and the bubbling stream winding its way past the site.

By the time they reluctantly gathered up their trash and drove home, evening shadows cast fantastic patterns on the road. The sky was alight with rose, gold, and purple clouds. The same colors bathed the Scotts' yellow house with its white shutters and blooming flowers. "Come in for a cool drink," Anne invited. "In spite of all the juice and water we took, I'm parched."

The enthusiastic troop eagerly followed her inside. Juli kicked off her tennis shoes, dangled them from one hand, and headed for her bedroom.

"Check the answering machine, will you, Juli?" Dad called.

"Sure." She entered the den and hit Play. Amy Hilton's voice sounded upset: "Juli, have Ted call me the instant you get back."

"She could at least say please and thank you," Juli muttered, listening for the next message. Amy again. And again.

Every message on the tape was from Amy. Each sounded more hysterical. Juli raced for the kitchen where family and friends stood holding iced glasses of lemonade. "Ted, Amy wants you to call. She left a bunch of messages."

Ted's face turned white. He set his half-empty glass on the counter, raced to the phone, and punched in the numbers. "Amy? Are you all right? Stop crying, will you? I can't understand. Is it Mom or Dad? No? Then what?" A long silence followed. No one in the kitchen spoke.

Juli glanced at Shannon. Her friend's Irish eyes looked more gray than blue. Oh, no. Shannon didn't need any more stress.

When Ted came back he looked both relieved and shocked. "Amy got her car out of the shop this morning. She parked it in the driveway, as usual. Mom made her do a bunch of housework, so she couldn't go anywhere until this afternoon. Sometime between this morning and a few hours ago, someone slashed all four tires." He shook his head as if to clear it of fuzziness. "Weird. We've never had trouble in our neighborhood, except kid stuff. You know, little kids ringing the bell and taking off before we come to the door."

"Why would anyone pull that kind of stunt in the middle of the day?" Juli gasped. "Wouldn't they be afraid of being seen?" A new thought hit her. "Was there any other damage—to your house, or to Amy's car itself?"

Ted shook his head, blue eyes more puzzled than ever. "Just the tires. The way our driveway's built, we can't see parked cars from any of our windows. Trees on both sides of us give privacy and the house across the street is built so a blank side faces us. Anyone driving by can see in, but how much attention do you pay to people in yards? You automatically assume they live there."

Shannon's eyes filled with sympathy. Juli's warm nature responded when her friend said, "Amy loves her car. She must be devastated."

Ted glared. "Furious is more like it. I don't blame her. There's no excuse for deliberately destroying other people's property." He sighed. "Sorry to break up the party, but I need to get home. Are you ready, Dave?" Ted clenched his right hand and pounded it into his left palm, then ran his fingers through his short brown hair and sighed again. A wobbly grin planted itself on his lips. "I've been beefing about not having a car. Right now, it doesn't seem like such a big deal."

"In other words, it's better to have no car at all than to have one with slashed tires," Dave solemnly said.

Ted bristled. "No way! I'd take my sister's Mustang, vandalism and all, if it were offered to me."

"Who wouldn't?" Shannon put in.

Before leaving, Dave managed to whisper to Juli, "Looks like Scott and Gilmore are back in business. See you tomorrow, fellow P.I."

"Sure." She and Shannon walked the boys to Dave's Mustang. A few minutes later she watched the Rileys and their van drive out of sight, then slowly turned and went back into the house. Dad and Mom had moved to the living room. Juli dropped to the floor and sat cross-legged. "How come for every high there's a low?" she complained. "Just when Shannon is getting it together, Amy's car is trashed. Not trashed, exactly. Wonder why whoever did it slashed the tires but didn't hurt the rest of the car?"

Gary Scott grimaced. "Who knows." His gray eyes looked dark. "No matter how much criminologists learn about warped minds, there are always unanswered questions. This is obviously one of them."

Anne Scott's smooth forehead puckered. "Juli, does Amy have enemies? I don't mean just people she annoys" —her blue eyes twinkled—"I know she can be a pain, but do you know of anyone who hates her enough to do something like this?"

Juli thought about it a long time before she said, "I don't think so." She concentrated hard. "Some of the girls who don't get picked for the cheerleading squad are naturally disappointed and jealous, but. . ." Her voice trailed off.

Gary Scott became all police officer. "You don't think any of them are vindictive enough to try and get back at Amy by attacking something she loves, do you? What about their families? Remember some of the cases over the past few years: Several fanatical persons have actually attacked the opposition in order for their relatives or friends to win competitions."

Juli felt sick. "I don't know a lot of the parents, Dad. You don't really think one of them would do something like this, do you?"

"I hope not, but we can't rule out the possibility." He leaned back in his chair.

Juli caught the tired note in his voice before her mother protested, "You aren't thinking about getting mixed up in this, are you, Gary? There are plenty of on-duty officers to handle it. It isn't your job."

"Preventing vicious behavior is everyone's job, but no, I don't intend to get involved. I'm on leave, remember?" Dad grinned and yawned. "I think I'll head for bed. What about you two?"

Juli got up from the floor. "Go ahead, Mom. I'll rinse the glasses and stick them in the dishwasher."

"Thanks." Anne smiled and followed her husband down the hall to their room.

It didn't take long to clean up and shower. Soon Juli crawled into bed and leaned back against her pillow. "I didn't realize how tense I was about Shannon facing her 'dragon' until right now," she told a bright-eyed Clue. A gigantic yawn made her wonder if she'd dislocated her jaw. One quick prayer later, she fell asleep, only to dream of Amy, her red Mustang, and shadowy figures Juli couldn't identify, no matter how hard she tried to see their faces.

Sunday morning dawned bright and beautiful. Juli checked out her closet and decided on a full-skirted cotton print dress. A hint of white collar added freshness. Shannon and her father arrived to accompany them. She wore a simple pink cotton skirt and t-shirt. Anne Scott greeted

Shannon with, "You look charming, second daughter." The compliment brought wild roses to smooth cheeks that had been pale too long.

Shannon hugged Mom and held her off to look admiringly at her tailored blue linen. "So do you. Blue is certainly your color."

"Just what I always say," Gary Scott approved. He dropped a kiss on Mom's tastefully arranged brownish-blond hair. "I love you all the time, and in any color, as long as it's blue."

"Typical man," Anne retorted, even though a blush colored her fair skin and told a more or less interested world that she loved her husband's teasing.

"Church is great, but I almost hate going this morning," Juli confessed to Shannon just before they followed the Scotts and Sean up the walk a little later.

"Juli Scott, how can you say such an awful thing?" Shannon looked at her with accusing eyes.

"Shhh. Keep your voice down." Juli glanced both ways to make sure no one was listening. "It's just that Amy will go on and on about her troubles—"

"Blather," Shannon helpfully supplied.

"Right." Julie shifted weight from one white sandal to the other. "I'm really sorry her car got vandalized, but you know how she is."

"I do," Shannon admitted as they walked through the front door of the church.

"Do what?" asked Ted, who had popped up behind

them; Dave was a few steps behind.

"Shannon thinks we'll be late if we don't go right in," Juli hastily told the boys. "How's Amy? Is she feeling better?"

Ted fell in step with Shannon, leaving Juli to walk beside Dave down the hall to the senior high classroom. "She's Amy-ish." Ted's knowing grin shouted loud and clear that even though he loved his twin, it didn't prevent him from seeing her faults. "All I've heard all morning is complaints about her being picked on." A trill of familiar laughter stopped Ted so suddenly, Juli nearly bumped into him. "Well, I'll be!" He stared at his sister, who stood just outside the classroom door. Amy, far from being the pouting girl Juli and Shannon had expected, was anything but. All smiles, she had never looked prettier. An obviously new and expensive pastel blue outfit embroidered with tiny flowers set off her blond curls and the pale blue eyes that sparkled like raindrops in sunlight.

Juli used her elbow to nudge Shannon in the ribs. The reason for Amy's changed mood stood smiling down at the tiny blond. "T-D-S-C," Shannon hissed in Juli's ear.

Juli bit back a nervous giggle. Translated, Shannon's message meant tall, dark, and super cool. No wonder Amy fluttered like a moth and gazed up into the newcomer's face with a positively awed expression. In spite of Juli's feelings for Dave Gilmore, she couldn't help experiencing a little thrill when Brett Jones looked down at her with dark eyes that smiled straight into her heart.

"Brett's eighteen, a senior, and will be attending Hill-crest," Amy announced. She also shot a warning *I-saw-him-first-so-don't-get-any-ideas* look at the other girls.

"Isn't it kind of late in the year to be transferring? Especially when you're a senior?" Shannon asked. If the new boy impressed her, it didn't show.

"Yes, but that's the way it goes sometimes." Brett hunched shoulders that made Juli think of the guys in ads for muscle-building. He turned another irresistible smile from Shannon to Julie, and back to Amy. One silky dark eyebrow went up. "I can see now it won't be so bad after all."

CHAPTER 7

For the first time in ages Juli found it hard to concentrate on the Sunday school lesson. Her mood was unusual; she felt strange without being able to explain why. It certainly had nothing to do with the quality of the class. Kareem Thompson, their senior high teacher and youth leader, brought so much enthusiasm to his teaching that even Amy Hilton couldn't help being challenged!

In his late twenties, Kareem's teeth gleamed white against his dark skin. His face shone with love for the Lord. *No wonder,* Juli thought. *God did so much for him.*

She swallowed a lump in her throat, remembering her teacher's story. A missionary and his wife found the child Kareem huddled near the lifeless bodies of his family in a war-torn African country after a massacre. No one knew how he had survived. Months and miles of red tape and restrictions later, the missionaries were allowed to adopt Kareem and bring him to the United States.

"The Thompsons saved my life," Kareem told his class the first time he and his soft-spoken wife, Jasmine, met with the students. "They gave me their name and became my parents. My heavenly Father did more. He made me His child and saved my soul. Even if I serve Him all my life, I can never repay Him."

"What does 'Kareem' mean?" someone asked.

The young man's expressive dark eyes sparkled. "It is Arabic for 'noble; exalted.' But my mother taught me it is God who is noble and to be exalted."

"You knew about God before you came to America?" Amy blurted out. Juli wanted to squash her.

"Oh, yes." Kareem looked surprised. "The Thompsons had visited our village many times. God called two of our young men to become missionaries to America." A pool of silence formed, then Kareem laughed. "I see by your faces the idea of God calling Africans to minister in America sounds foreign. Not so. People from my country have much to give to those who live here."

The class certainly found it was true, at least as far as Kareem was concerned. They'd never had a teacher who brought Bible stories more alive than the earnest young man whose life God had saved. Today was no exception. They discussed the parable of the Good Samaritan.

"The story is found in Luke 10, and we've all heard it a thousand times," Kareem told them. "Now let's see what it really means. Does anyone know why the Jews despised the Samaritans?"

"Because they weren't Jews," someone offered.

Everyone laughed, including Kareem. "Right. Hatred between the Jews and Samaritans was so bad that when they met, they fought one another."

"Nice guys," Brett Jones put in. He grinned at Juli, whose heart thumped.

"I need six volunteers to role-play the story," Kareem said. "We won't pay attention to male or female." He didn't wait for hands, but pointed to three girls and three boys, including Brett. "Unless you'd rather not," the teacher added.

"I don't mind." Brett swaggered to the front.

Kareem quickly assigned roles: victim, robber, priest; Levite, Samaritan, innkeeper. He chose Brett to be the victim. "All right. Let's go over the story. Our victim is Jewish. He is attacked, robbed, and beaten. A priest comes along, his mind on performing sacrifices at the temple. If he stops to help a wounded man, it will make him both late and unclean. He passes by.

"The Levite is a member of a well-respected tribe. He sees the fallen man but also passes by. Then a Samaritan comes. He bandages the victim's wounds. He puts him on a donkey, takes him to an inn, and pays for his care. He also tells the innkeeper he will return and pay any extra expenses."

Kareem told the six up front, "I want you to close your eyes, put yourselves inside the parts you've been assigned, then tell the class how you—as the victim, Samaritan, and so on—felt during your part of the story.

Brett was the first to speak. "First I felt scared I'd die, then angry because people of my own race looked at me and ignored my cries for help. When the Samaritan came, I knew I was history." He took a backward step, obviously enjoying the role. "I couldn't believe it when the guy helped me!"

"Good, Brett. Thanks," Kareem praised. "What about the rest of you?"

"I was glad to get the money," the "robber" said. "Who cares about a Jew?"

"I have duties and responsibilities," the "priest" haughtily reported. "No one can expect me to stop for every unfortunate person along the highway."

"Same here," the "Levite" chimed in. "I'm an important man. Besides, there was no one around to see that I didn't stop."

The "innkeeper" declared, "Jew, Samaritan, who cares as long as they pay?"

The "Samaritan" admitted she felt reluctant at first, but just couldn't pass by.

When the players took their seats, the class cheered, but their teacher had a real zinger for them. "Suppose this happened today? What if I'm in downtown Bellingham and gang members beat me and leave me on the street? An African-American minister comes by. He doesn't stop. A respected African-American businesswoman also walks on by. She pretends not to see. Then a member of a white supremacist group approaches me. I look at his shaved head, camouflage clothing, and a suspicious bulge under his jacket that tells me he's carrying a weapon. Trust me, I am one scared victim! I start saying my prayers.

"The man gives me first aid. He calls a cab and takes me to the nearest emergency room. When he finds out I don't have insurance, he signs an affidavit making himself responsible for whatever medical care I need."

John Foster raised his hand. "That makes it a lot more real."

"Yes, it does," Kareem agreed. "My challenge to you is the same as the one Jesus gave the lawyer who came to test him: 'Which of these three do you think was neighbor to the man who fell into the hands of robbers?' " He smiled again. "Class dismissed."

A buzz of conversation followed. Juli nodded at the appropriate places, even contributed enough so the others wouldn't suspect anything out of the ordinary. She also determined to listen to every word of Pastor Johnson's sermon, but her mind wandered in spite of her good intentions. What was wrong with her, anyway? She'd come to church to worship God, hadn't she? Why *wasn't* she?

Church ended and the congregation spilled out into the parking lot. Amy breathed to Juli, "Brett is so-o-o good-looking! He must be a Christian, too. He really listened in class and church." She smirked as though she had invented Brett Jones. "He also knew the story of the Good Samaritan."

"Yeah," Juli reluctantly agreed. "Of course, Kareem gave the facts."

Amy's smirk changed to a pout. She glared and started to flounce off, but stopped when Dave Gilmore said, "Jones has good taste in cars."

Amy glanced in the direction Dave was looking, squealed, and zeroed in on the visitor like a well-directed rocket. "Talk about coincidences! I've been wondering who owned the Mustang I saw at Pizza Palace a couple of weeks ago. Is it a graduation gift?"

Brett turned toward the admiring group surrounding the white Mustang. He looked bewildered. "Yes, but I don't know what you mean about a pizza palace?"

"Not *a* pizza palace. *The* Pizza Palace," Amy gushed. "They have the greatest food anywhere. You'll have to go with us sometime."

Brett gave her an amused look. "Sure. I can eat pizza seven days a week." He glanced at Molly, Shannon, and last of all at Juli. His smile widened, and she felt her heart give a little lurch.

"I'm sure it was that car I saw," Amy persisted. "I have a Mustang of my own, so I check out all the others I see."

"And their drivers," Juli couldn't help whispering to Shannon, who grinned.

Brett shook his dark head. "I only got the car a few days ago."

Amy hated being wrong about the slightest thing. Now she refused to let the subject go. "Maybe someone had your car at the Pizza Palace before you got it."

"It didn't come from here." He slid into the spotless Mustang, started the engine, and called out, "See you tomorrow." But his parting look was aimed at Juli.

After dinner Juli went to her bedroom and changed into jeans shorts and an oversized white shirt. She curled up on the bed. Writing in her journal always helped clear the fog from her brain. She gave Clue an absentminded pat and began putting down words—slowly at first, then faster.

> *I can't blame my lack of concentration on the lesson today. It was even better than usual. Kareem does such a great job! Thanks, Lord, for sending him to our class. I can't blame lack of sleep, or worry, or even the gorgeous day, either.*

Juli thought of how all during the excellent portrayal of the story she had only listened with one ear. Sighing, she picked up her pen and went on.

> *Okay, God, I'll be honest. I don't want Shannon or Dave or the others—especially Dave!—to know, but the real reason I didn't get as much out of class today is Brett Jones. He sat by Amy, but I sure received more than my fair share of dazzling smiles. He really is TDSC—tall, dark, and super cool.*

I still like Dave, a whole lot. Brett Jones means nothing to me, does he? It's probably because he's older. Or that I'd like to show Amy that every new boy, in this case young man, who comes along isn't her private property.

Juli crossed out the last sentence. Putting things like that on paper made her feel shallow, the trait she disliked most in Amy!

Sorry, Lord,

Before she could continue, a light tap sounded on her partially opened door. Shannon's face appeared in the opening. "Juli?"

"Come on in," she called, tossing her journal onto her desk next to Clue. Unlike some parents, Gary and Anne respected their daughter's privacy. She knew neither would read her journal, even if she left it wide open and in plain sight. "What's up?"

Shannon giggled. What a difference Saturday had made. Her face glowed above a yellow knit shirt and matching shorts. "You should be. Up and out. How come you're playing hermit on a day like this?" She waved toward Juli's open window. "I rode my bike over. Let's go for a bike ride, okay?"

"Sounds great." Juli scrambled off her bed. A few minutes later, they headed down the shady, tree-lined street.

"Some of the kids think it isn't cool to ride bikes unless they're trail bikes," Shannon commented. "I intend to keep riding my bike until I'm gray and old. Or at least until I can no longer pedal."

"You mean 'old and gray.' " Juli expertly swerved to avoid a boy darting in and out on a skateboard.

"Picky, picky," Shannon complained.

Juli replied by putting on a burst of speed and passing the Irish girl. She glanced back over her shoulder and laughed. In the lightning second of inattention, disaster struck.

"Juli, look out!" Shannon screamed.

It was too late. The front wheel of the bicycle collided with a furiously barking beast that loomed big as a house in front of Juli. Girl, bike, and dog went down in a heap of wildly spinning wheels, waving arms, and legs.

Shannon screeched to a stop inches short of hitting them. She leaped from her bike and raced to the pileup. "Stay under the bicycle," she shouted to Juli. "You crashed into a rottenweiler. Help, someone!"

Juli heard the deep baying of the dog. A rottweiler? Fear spurted into the fallen girl's brain. "Run, Shannon! Rottweilers can be dangerous!"

The Irish girl refused to budge. White-faced but determined, she ignored the dog's deep baying and seized the chain dangling from his collar. "No one's going to hurt you," she told him. The rottweiler didn't move. Worse, his barking increased until it could have drowned out a stadium of fans gone mad over the victory of a favorite team.

Fear for her friend lent strength to Juli. Ignoring her scraped and bleeding hands and knees, she freed herself from the tangle and got to her feet. She grabbed for the chain, but the dog sidestepped and continued to howl.

"What's going on here? What are you doing to my dog?" an angry voice demanded. A mighty grip jerked the chain from Shannon's desperate hands. "Down, Bruno." The man stroked the dog's coarse black hair. With a woof that sounded like a rumble of thunder, Bruno subsided. The furious owner whirled toward the girls. "I asked you a question." He looked at Juli's bleeding knees and hands. "Don't try and tell me Bruno did that. He doesn't bite. Ever."

"With that bark, he doesn't have to!" Juli snorted. Nervous reaction started at her toes and moved up. By the time it reached her throat, it changed to laughter.

"I fail to see anything vaguely amusing about your persecuting my dog," the man snapped. "What happened, anyway?" He moved his hands over Bruno's body. "It doesn't appear he's hurt."

The man's lack of concern pushed Shannon beyond emotional limits. Her voice rose until passersby couldn't help hearing. "My friend is hurt. She could have been hurt a lot worse." Shannon clenched her hands behind her back. "No thanks to you that she wasn't. The law says animals are to be kept under control at all times. You just broke the law by letting your rottenweiler off the leash."

The man gaped at Shannon's pronunciation of rottweiler, but Shannon wasn't through. "That's bad enough, but roaring up here and accusing us of doing something to your dog is disgusting!" She paused for breath.

"That's telling him, little lady." A burly driver of a delivery truck jumped out, arms crossed belligerently. "I'm a witness, if you girls wanta sue him."

Juli's face flamed with embarrassment, but she managed a smile for their champion. "It was an accident. No lawsuits. I'm glad the dog wasn't hurt."

The rottweiler's owner just turned on his heel and stalked away.

The helpful driver muttered something under his breath. Juli suspected it was more emphatic than elegant. His strong hands straightened the bent fenders of her bike. He produced a first aid kit, cleaned her abrasions, and bandaged them. "Need a ride home?" he wanted to know.

"No, thanks. I can call my dad." Juli moved her knees. They were getting stiff. She hid her pain and told the driver, "Thank you for being a Good Samaritan."

"Who, me?" The man turned bright red, but looked pleased. "Anytime." He crawled back in his truck and drove away with a cheerful wave of his hand.

"Do you realize we were just involved in a modern parable?" Shannon asked.

Juli gritted her teeth and limped toward a nearby bench. "Just call Dad, will you, please? The best part of this story will definitely be THE END."

CHAPTER 8

The day after Juli's bicycle spill, she was stiff and sore all over. She limped to classes, painfully aware of her scraped knees and elbows—and that every student at Hillcrest High must know Juli Scott collided with a dog! Gossip Queen Amy had made a very big deal out of the accident. Juli scowled and complained to Shannon on the way to the cafeteria, "She acts like I hit an elephant or rhinoceros or something. It's humiliating."

"I'm sorry I ever told her," Shannon apologized.

Juli managed a weak grin. "Not much else you could say when she asked why I was limping. Come on; let's go eat and hope Amy keeps quiet for once."

"Fat chance." Shannon looked sympathetic and suggested helpfully, "Maybe she'll choke on a hot dog." She immediately covered her mouth, but a giggle slipped out. "Sorry. Bad choice of words."

Juli gave her a look. "Right. I won't hold my breath

waiting for Amy Hilton to step out of the spotlight." She gingerly flexed one knee, then the other, glad for the gauze bandages that kept her skirt from brushing the abrasions. Her body loosened up when she walked between classes, then stiffened when she sat.

"Amy doesn't always eat in the cafeteria." Shannon tucked her red t-shirt more firmly into the waistband of her black jeans.

"She'll be there," Juli predicted.

"Can you feel it in your aching bones?" Shannon asked.

"More like in my aching knees," Juli told her.

Amy was there, all right. The pretty bottle-blond, as the girls secretly called her, sat at a table with Ted, Dave, John, Molly, and. . .

"Do you see what I see?" Shannon pretended to stagger. Her right hand clutched her chest in the general region of her heart.

Juli's own heart fluttered as rapidly as Amy's heavily darkened eyelashes fluttered at the boy beside her.

"How come Brett Jones, mighty senior, descends to sit with a group of lowly sophs?" Shannon asked in a stage whisper.

"That's *condescends*," Juli told her. "Descends means to come down."

"It's coming down for seniors to associate with underclassmen, isn't it?" Shannon defended herself.

"Does my hair look all right?" Juli swiped at it.

"It's fine. Besides, Dave Gilmore is so crazy about you

he won't care if your hair is messed up," the Irish girl teased.

"No, but Brett Jones will." The words slipped out before Juli could stop them.

Shannon, who had been reaching for a tray, stopped with one hand in midair. She ignored the boy behind them who yelled, "Hurry it up, will you?" Her Irish eyes opened wide. "Brett Jones! Are you kidding?"

"Shhh. Get your tray and move on," Juli hissed. She gave her friend a little shove.

Shannon obeyed like a zombie. She managed to grab napkins, utensils, and move ahead. She also lowered her voice at least an octave. "Juli, do you like Brett? What about Dave?"

Juli felt a furious tide of red surge into her face. Would she ever outgrow the childish habit of blushing? "I didn't say I liked Brett, did I?"

"You didn't have to." The accusing look in Shannon's face made Juli angry.

"It's not like I'm married to Dave, or anything," she said through gritted teeth. "I'm just his girlfriend *pro tem*."

"For the time being," Shannon translated. In an obvious effort to settle Juli down, she glanced at her watch and went into an Irish brogue routine. "Mercy me, but the time is for bein' late."

"So *Erin go bragh*—Ireland forever—to you, too," Juli muttered, but she couldn't help laughing when Shannon grinned at her.

Between Amy's gushing, Brett Jones's admiring glances, and Dave's unusual silence, it didn't take Juli long to lose her appetite. She picked at the macaroni and cheese, wondering why she had selected it. "Any food that makes a fork bounce when you stab it isn't fit for human consumption," she announced.

Bright-eyed Molly laughed. Her freckles shone brighter than ever and her brown eyes glowed. "Maybe it's fighting back."

Everyone laughed but Amy, who disliked not being the focus of attention. "Speaking of fighting back, did you think the owner of the dog you hit was going to bite you, Juli?" She laced her fingers. "I'd simply die if attacked by a huge beast."

Juli sent Shannon an imploring glance. Her friend quickly responded by saying, "Juli wasn't attacked by the rottenweiler. She just collided with him."

"The *what?*" Brett Jones dropped his spoon. His good-looking jaw dropped.

Amy leaped back into control of the conversation. "That's just one of what we call 'Rileyisms.' Shannon mispronounces words and misquotes phrases."

Juli tuned out the elaborate explanation of Rileyisms that threatened to become an all-lunch-break monologue. She stared at the macaroni and cheese. Why didn't someone tell Amy how silly she was? Resentment filled Juli. So much for trying to like Ted's twin. She glanced up. He looked as bored as the rest of the group around the table.

That did it. Why should they listen to Amy blather on and on every day? Juli interrupted the tinkly voice laughing at her own wit. "Brett, would you like to be part of our church youth group's Adopt-a-Grandparent program?" She knew she was being rude but didn't care. Besides, the relief in the faces around her helped justify her changing the subject. So did the look on Amy's face.

They spent the rest of their lunch break discussing the Adopt-a-Grandparent program. Brett agreed to participate in it. "When I have the time," he added.

"Do you have a part-time job or something?" John Foster asked.

"Yeah." He gathered his dishes and grinned at them. "I have to run. See you."

"See you," the others chorused, with Amy's shrill voice louder than the rest.

The minute the girls got on the bus that night and found a seat, the Irish girl broke out laughing. "I know it's mean, but did you see Amy's face when you broke into her recitation? She looked like a cat that swallowed a sour mouse!"

"I've never had anyone bring out the worst in me like Amy," Juli confided.

"Me, either. Amy is another Nellie Oleson. You know, in *Little House on the Prairie*. She drove Laura Ingalls crazy."

"I remember." Juli fished in her backpack for a tissue and wiped her eyes.

"The difference is, Nellie at least had some excuse.

Her mother and her brother Willie were just as bad. Amy doesn't have that excuse."

"No, she doesn't. Mrs. Hilton is so nice, and Ted is, uh, Ted. . ." A smile lit up Shannon's face and lingered in her eyes.

"I know." Juli sighed. "Shannon, I know we're supposed to be glad when new kids come to church, but I wish Brett Jones hadn't come to Bellingham. He's disturbing." She thought of the way the new senior's dark gaze had rested on her so many times during lunch. "If I really, truly, like Dave—"

"Which you do," Shannon said when Juli hesitated.

"Of course." Juli indignantly told her. "It's just that Brett is so different."

"So senior," Shannon put in. "He makes my heart beat a little faster, too. It's something about the way he smiles. Brett makes it personal and exciting, as if you're the most important girl in the world." She grinned and quickly added, "Even when you know he's smiling the same way at all the other girls."

But not as often, Juli's rebellious heart whispered.

The whisper stayed with her until bedtime, along with a question: Suppose Brett asked her out? Would she go? Her heart thundered at the idea, and not just from the excitement of a possible date with a senior. What would Dave Gilmore say? Dave, the boy she had liked since junior high. Dave, partner and fellow investigator in the unofficial firm of Scott and Gilmore, P.I.s. Dave, who had risked who knew what in order to save Shannon.

Gradually Dave's blond-brown hair and honest blue gaze replaced the image of laughing dark eyes beneath well-styled dark hair. Juli fell asleep smiling. Why worry over something that might never happen?

The insistent shrill of the telephone roused her from deep sleep. Juli glanced at her digital clock. The red numerals were at 6:30. Who'd be calling this time of day? A wrong number, maybe? She strained her ears to hear Dad's voice. All she could make out was a mumble, too long to be answering a wrong number. Wide awake, Juli bounced out of bed and met her father at the door of her room.

"It was Sean Riley, Juli. Don't panic. Shannon is all right." Yet the grave look in Gary Scott's gray eyes showed all was not well on this spring morning. "Get dressed. She wants us to come to the hospital."

Juli felt like someone had dropped a house on her. "Is it Grand?" she choked out. Juli clenched her hands until the nails bit into her palms. A little voice inside pleaded, *Please, God, not that. Shannon's been through enough.*

"The Rileys are all right." Dad put his hands on her shoulders. "It's Ted Hilton. He's been in some kind of accident. Let's hope it isn't serious."

"Ted!" Juli sagged against the door frame for support. Her bare toes curled and dug into the soft rug. Her eyes were open wide. "When? Where? How did Shannon find out?"

"Don't waste time asking questions." Gary tightened his hold, then released Juli and strode down the hall.

Juli fumbled her way into jeans, a shirt, and sandals. She ran a comb through her hair, shoved it back, and caught it with a scrunchie. A quick brushing of her teeth and she was ready.

Mom didn't go with them. "Being late for school if you're a student is one thing," she said. "Teachers being late is another." Her attractive face looked concerned. "I'll be praying, though. It's the best thing anyone can do."

Juli agreed. Buckled securely in her seat belt, she listened to Dad tell what he knew while driving to the hospital. "Amy Hilton evidently called just a few minutes before Sean phoned us. She was crying, but not hysterical."

"Which means it can't be too awful," Juli thankfully said. "Amy isn't all that calm in emergency situations." Realization and shame flooded through her. Less than twenty-hour hours ago, she had wanted to show Amy up for being a moron. Now the other girl's twin brother lay in the hospital. Shallow as she was, Amy did love Ted. Juli remembered how she herself had felt when Dad was gone. And when she'd been separated from Shannon. Tears of compassion sprang from the deep well inside her. For the gazillionth time she vowed to try harder to like Amy. Not only for Ted's sake, but because she knew Jesus wanted her to. She stared at her hands, wordlessly praying for Ted until they swung into the visitors' parking lot.

Gary and Juli found the Rileys and Hiltons gathered

in the waiting room outside the emergency ward. To Juli's surprise, Amy flew to her and flung her arms around Juli's waist. "I'm so glad you came! I knew Shannon would, but I forgot to tell her to bring you."

Juli stared at Shannon over Amy's tousled blond head. Never had the smaller girl been more appealing or more vulnerable. Her face shone with nothing more than soap and water. Her light blue, tear-filled eyes cried out for help. Her arms tightened around Juli. "It's so awful." A torrent of tears started and Juli involuntarily stroked Amy's mussed-up hair.

"What exactly happened?" Gary Scott asked.

Mr. Hilton, a haggard older edition of his son, shook his head. "As near as we can piece things together, Ted went running before school. An unidentified driver hit him and took off."

"Does he run a lot in the morning?"

Juli detected a suspicious note in her father's voice. It started her nerves twanging like broken strings on a guitar.

"Yes. Why do you ask?" Mrs. Hilton's expression changed from concern to horror. She clutched at her throat. "You don't think—you can't think this was anything more than a freak accident!"

"Police officers, even those on leave, are suspicious critters," Dad said lightly. "It's probably exactly what you called it. On the other hand, Mrs. Hilton, I understand there was some trouble with Amy's Mustang? I believe Juli said someone slashed the tires?"

Horror filled Mrs. Hilton's eyes. Amy gasped, tore herself free from Juli, and ran to her mother. "It's just a coincidence," she cried fiercely. "It can't be anything else. Why would anyone want to hurt Ted?"

That was exactly what Dad had asked Juli after the tire-slashing incident, Juli remembered. She noticed how keen his gray eyes became, but before he could reply, an on-duty emergency room doctor marched into the waiting area. "Who belongs to the young man involved in the hit-and-run accident?" he demanded.

"I'm Ted's father. This is his mother and our daughter, Amy," Mr. Hilton said. "How is he, doctor?"

"Badly shaken. A broken right leg. No signs of internal bleeding. A bump on his head that doesn't appear serious, but I'm ordering Xrays to make sure."

Juli couldn't help contrasting the doctor's methodical listing of Ted's injuries with Dr. Marlowe's far more compassionate treatment of patients and their families. She felt sorry for the Hiltons, and indignant at the lack of bedside manner. A closer examination showed the attending physician's red-rimmed eyes and the fatigue in his face. Juli's indignation died. Emergency must have had a bad night. Who was she to condemn the doctor for not being at his best?

As if to confirm Juli's thoughts, the doctor yawned. "Sorry." He gave them an apologetic grin. "It's been one long night." His weary smile made a difference. "All Ted's signs are good. Unless something shows on the Xrays, he will be up and hopping soon. Literally. We'll get him into a cast, and before you know it, he will be home and back to school. No more running for a while, though."

"May we see him?" Shannon whispered.

"Relatives only. The rest of you may visit this afternoon or evening."

Juli found Shannon's obvious disappointment hard to bear. She put her arm around her friend's shoulders. "We'll come back after school," she promised.

"At least he's going to be all right," Shannon quavered before she repeated Amy's question. "Do you understand why anyone would want to hurt Ted?"

A few weeks earlier, Juli had felt she never wanted to face another mystery. Now she felt something begin to stir inside her. Feelings of excitement and anticipation, all mixed up with loyalty to Ted and Shannon, even to Amy. "No, but I'll tell you one thing, Shannon Riley. We are going to find out. When we do, someone is going to be *verrry* sorry!"

CHAPTER 9

Even a broken leg couldn't get brown-haired Ted Hilton down. When Juli, Dave, and Shannon arrived in the two-bed hospital room during visitors' hours, Ted seemed himself, with the addition of a cast on his leg and a bandaged head. He occupied the bed nearest the window. The second stood empty and waiting. A pot of brightly blooming azaleas sat on a wall shelf. Shannon put the bouquet of roses she and Juli had brought from the Scott garden next to it.

Ted sniffed appreciatively. "Thanks. They sure smell good."

Juli couldn't wait a moment longer. "So what happened?"

"I wish I knew!" Ted's lips twisted into a crooked grin. "One minute I'm running along listening to the birds sing. I come to a corner, check both ways, and start across the street. Bang! Something smashes into me. I fly through the air and hit the ground hard. The next thing I know, I wake up in the hospital."

"You didn't see or hear *anything?*" Dave sounded disappointed.

Ted closed his eyes and concentrated. "No. At least nothing I can remember." His eyelids popped open and one hand flew to his bandaged head. "Sorry. It hurts to think. The police were in earlier to take my statement." Ted made a face. "I didn't have much for them, either. They told me not to push it. If anything is hiding in my brain cells, they say it may come back unexpectedly. Especially if it's important." He fell silent. A strange expression came across his face.

"What?" Shannon asked.

Ted moved restlessly against his pillows. "The police said hit-and-runs are common. Some things about mine aren't."

Juli smelled a mystery. "Like what?" she demanded.

"Spoken like a true detective," Ted teased. "Okay, Madame Sleuth. Or is it Sleuthess?" Juli groaned and he held up one hand. "We have some facts that are baffling the police." Ted ticked them off on his fingers.

"*One*. The street where I run is close to being deserted that early in the morning. *Two*. I always double-check both ways for cars before crossing. This morning, zip. So where did the car or truck or whatever that hit me come from?"

"Maybe it was parked, waiting for you," Juli offered.

Shannon gasped in horror, but Ted just looked disgusted.

"Some maniac is parked, waiting for me to show up so he can hit me and take off? Get real, Juli."

She defended the theory her father had planted in her mind when he talked with Mr. and Mrs. Hilton early that morning. "It's no big secret that you run mornings, is it?"

"No, but—"

"Stop it, Juli!" Shannon cried. She clenched her hands. Every trace of color left her face. "If what you're saying is true, it means Ted is being stalked."

The ugly word hung in the quiet hospital room like poisonous fog. After a few moments Ted triumphantly announced, "Impossible. Number three on the list of things that don't make sense is how I got here."

"How *did* you?" Dave's blue eyes darkened.

"I don't know. The police don't, either. I overheard some officers talking outside my door." Ted started to sit up but fell back with a moan. "My head spins when I move too fast."

"Maybe we should leave and come back later," Shannon suggested.

Juli felt torn between curiosity and Ted's welfare. "Good idea," she reluctantly agreed.

"What? And not hear the most mysterious part of all?" Ted tormented. "I'm okay as long as I stay put."

"Then stay put, tell us, and we'll get out of here," Shannon ordered. The glint in her eyes and firm set of her chin showed she meant business.

"Yes, boss," Ted said meekly. "*Three*. So far, the police

haven't found even one person in the neighborhood who saw or heard anything, let alone brought me to the hospital."

Shannon's eyes looked like blue-gray saucers. "You mean you didn't come in an ambulance?"

In the split second after Ted shook his head, Juli had a wild thought. "Then if a neighbor didn't bring you, or an ambulance, it means—"

"Right." Ted clenched his hands and shot his fists into the air. *"The only person who could logically have delivered my unconscious body to Emergency is the hit-and-run driver!"*

Shannon stared. "That's insane. What kind of person hits someone, leaves the scene of the accident, and returns to play Good Samaritan? It doesn't make sense. No wonder the police aren't able to make heads or tails of it!"

Juli looked perplexed. "Hold it, will you? There's something. . ." She paused. Excitement burst inside her like a handful of firecrackers. "Didn't we say the same thing when someone slashed the tires on Amy's car? We couldn't understand why the guilty person didn't wreck the paint or smash the windows. Is there a pattern here? A profile of someone who does bad things but has set an imaginary line, not to be crossed?"

A no-nonsense type nurse stepped into Ted's room. She jerked a thumb toward the open door and told the visitors in a voice as crisp as her pantsuit uniform, "Out. This is a hospital, not a visitors' center. This young man's had too many people in here."

Ted turned scarlet at the patronizing tone of the words "young man." "Give me a break, Kelly. It's just been Dad and Mom. Oh, yeah—Amy, too."

Another significant jerk of Kelly's thumb sent Ted's friends through the door, trying not to laugh at Ted's parting comment, "Come back when Kelly's in a better mood, okay?"

"Don't hold your breath," they heard the obviously competent nurse warn.

Shannon giggled all the way down the hall. "She may as well have added, 'And I don't mean perhaps.' Right?"

Dave howled. "*Maybe,* not perhaps."

"So maybe the nurse's bite is worse than her bark," Shannon retorted.

Dave laughed again and added, "We'd better pray Kelly never bites. Excuse me, but her bark is more than enough."

"Just like Juli's rottenweiler," Shannon observed. Her comment set her friends off again.

"He's not my rottweiler," Juli protested between laughing and gasping for air.

"Please, Shannon," Dave pleaded. "Three Rileyisms in a row are more than I can take. Hey, here's one for you. Seven days may make one week, but three days of Rileyisms make anyone weak."

Shannon stuck her nose in the air, but her eyes twinkled. "No way is that a Rileyism, Dave Gilmore. If you're going to move in on my territory, do it right."

Juli grabbed her aching sides, but her heart rejoiced. It was so good to have the old Shannon back. No, not the old Shannon. Her friend would never again be the innocent, trusting girl she had once been. Yet in her place was a Shannon of greater perception; a girl far less likely to be led astray.

That night at dinner, Juli faithfully reported the results of the hospital visit to her parents. Anne Scott shook her head in bewilderment. Gary said little. After dinner, he headed for the den and closed the door, alerting Mom and Juli to his need for privacy. His gray eyes flashed when he came back.

"Want to hear the latest?" he teased.

"Sure, if it isn't classified," Juli threw back at him. She grinned. Never in a million years would Dad pass on classified information to his family.

"Reporters already have the story," Gary said. "It will be on the late news. This is it in a nutshell. The police interviewed every person in the vicinity of Ted's accident. Unless someone's lying, and there's no evidence to indicate it, one of two things happened. Either a total stranger found Ted and took him to the hospital—that's highly unlikely—or the driver of the vehicle came back. The police are asking anyone who saw or heard anything suspicious to call a hot line."

Mom's pretty face showed concern. "Sometimes hit-and-run drivers do return," she said. "They panic, feel they have to get away, then reconsider."

"Not in this case." Gary's level gaze pinned itself on Juli's face.

"How can the police be sure?" she wanted to know, dreading the answer.

"Tire tracks. The car was headed north. It traveled across the center lane, then sharply back. The driver couldn't have been trying to avoid Ted by swerving. If Ted checked both ways, as he said, he had to be fairly close to the opposite curb. There's also something else."

Juli looked at him expectantly.

"It appears the car was parked by the right curb a little back of where Ted crossed. There's no way the driver could have failed to see your friend."

Juli felt sick. "So someone definitely tried to kill Ted." Shock waves ran through her.

Dad went on. "That's a possibility, except to our knowledge, no one has a reason to hate Ted Hilton that much. Other explanations include mistaken identity or a warning. Random is out. No one waits in a car in the hopes someone, anyone, will show up in the exact spot to become a victim at a time no witnesses are around." He looked at Juli sympathetically. "I'm afraid your friends the Hiltons are being targeted by an unknown person or persons."

The next day, Hillcrest High buzzed like a hundred beehives. Rumors flew "fast and thick," as Shannon described the talk.

"I can't believe it," Amy tearfully told the lunch bunch in the cafeteria. "I've heard everything from speculation that Ted is secretly a reformed gang member and the victim of former associates, to the theory he simply slipped and took a bad fall. I'm amazed someone hasn't blamed it on aliens."

Juli felt sorry for her. "Don't pay any attention to what people say. They'll find something or someone else to rip apart soon enough."

"I know." Amy looked disconsolate. "It just hurts so much in the meantime."

"Tell me about it," Shannon put in. "I've been there." She lowered her voice and softly said, "Don't forget to ask God for help. I wouldn't have made it through without Him."

Amy's lips quivered. "I have. Really and truly."

"The rest of us are praying for you and Ted. Your parents, too," John Foster gruffly told the troubled girl.

Brett Jones looked startled, but mumbled a quick, "Yeah." Juli had the feeling he hadn't spent a lot of time around kids who talked about praying.

For once, Amy's look held pure gratitude, without a trace of flirting or trying to win back the boy who had wised up to her real nature and chosen Molly Bowen for his girl. "Thanks, John. You too, Brett."

"All for one and one for us all," Shannon said.

"Another Rileyism?" Brett's dark eyes twinkled and he grinned at Juli. She knew Dave noticed by the scowl that appeared like magic.

Molly patted Amy's hand. "We're here for you," she promised.

"Thanks." Amy hastily rose and left the cafeteria. Was she thinking of all the times she'd snubbed Molly? Or was she too concerned over Ted to think at all? She must be, since she hadn't paid any more attention to Brett than to the others.

Juli looked at the red-haired girl whose face was sprinkled with freckles. The more she and Shannon hung out with Molly, the better they liked her. Both admired the fact she accepted herself for what she was, something Juli found hard to do. Competition meant nothing to Molly; but it meant a great deal to Shannon, and even more to Juli.

"I'm one of those average people statistics quote," Molly told them once when she slept over at Juli's. Her brown eyes sparkled with mischief. "You know the kind of student. Mr. Smiles takes ten minutes to remember who I am. I'm neither beautiful nor ugly. I'm not super cool or a troublemaker. I don't get 'A' grades or flunk. If I ever make a team or get elected to an office it will have to be when I get to heaven!" She laughed so contagiously the other girls joined in.

"You are so together," Juli exclaimed. "As long as it's true confessions time, I admit being first is really important to me."

"So do I," Shannon admitted with a thoughtful look in her eyes. "Or at least ahead of Juli. Molly, how can you. . ."

She broke off, obviously embarrassed.

A smile that showed inner beauty behind the freckles lit up Molly's face. "You're both so popular and talented you may find it hard to understand, but I really like being me—red hair, freckles, and average." She sobered and a shadow crept into her eyes. "I didn't when I was a kid and got called 'Carrots.' Then one day Dad and Mom sat me down and we talked."

"Really?" Juli leaned forward. "This is better than a *Guideposts* story."

Molly stared at her hands. "They asked me if I believed God made mistakes."

Shannon gulped. Juli took a quick breath.

Molly blinked and fiercely said, "I told them of course not!" The lips that so easily curved into a smile trembled. "I'll never forget Dad quietly telling me God made me just the way He wanted me, unique and special. He said God gave me what He knew would be best for me, Molly Bowen. No one else in the world could ever be exactly like me, any more than any two snowflakes are the same."

"That's pretty heavy for a kid," Juli murmured.

Molly displayed her pixie grin. "Yes. It took a long time for me to believe it, and a lot of focusing on what I could do instead of what I couldn't. So what if I only made 'C' grades, no matter how hard I tried? Instead of perfect report cards on the refrigerator, Mom posted pictures of the first successful cake Betty Crocker and I baked. She added snapshots of my dog after I washed him. She awarded and displayed blue ribbons lettered 'Best Bedroom Cleaner in Whatcom County,' 'Kindest Kid in the Neighborhood Today,' that kind of thing."

Shannon clapped her hands. "That is so neat!"

Molly wasn't finished. She tilted her head to one side. "Accepting the way I looked took longer. Dad galloped to the rescue like the hero in a TV western when I started comparing myself with the girls in *Seventeen*. He said I should always remember one thing: God liked my face well enough to give it to *His own child*." One tear escaped, and Molly whispered, "After that, it didn't matter what others thought." She waited for a moment. "I'm glad John Foster likes it, too."

"He certainly does," Shannon agreed. So did Juli, more thankful than ever that Molly had started coming to the church youth group. When her friends fell into a deep sleep, Juli felt for her journal and carried it to the bathroom. She wrote:

I want to be more like Molly. She is so real. So natural, Lord. Sometimes I can say like Molly did, "I really like being me," but not always. Molly isn't a fake, either. She's accepted herself as You accept her. It shows. I'm still trying, God. Thanks for making me special, too, and for being patient with me.

She thought for a long time, sighed and finally wrote,

Something awful is happening to Ted and Amy
and their parents. No one knows the truth except
You. Please take care of them and don't let all
this set Shannon back just when she is doing so
well. Good night, Lord. I love You.

The bell signaling the end of lunch break returned Juli's wandering mind to the present. She grabbed her tray and smiled at Molly. Dave walked her out of the cafeteria. "Wish something nice would happen," she wistfully told him when they started down the hall.

He grinned at her. His light brown hair that bleached to blond in summer looked so right above his tanned face. "I'm here."

"I know." Yet she couldn't help glancing back at Brett, who had announced since Ted wasn't there, he would walk Shannon to class. A second later, Juli wished she hadn't. She felt Dave stiffen. Uh-oh. Storm warnings. Great. The last thing she needed just now was another tough problem for which she had no solution.

CHAPTER 10

Mr. S. (for Samuel) Miles, fondly called Mr. Smiles behind his back, was the kind of administrator school boards dream of and feel lucky to find. His optimistic outlook and high expectations both inspired the school and helped Mr. Smiles handle times of difficulty.

The principal could also be tough when the occasion demanded. In spite of his willingness to give students a second chance, Hillcrest became one of the first zero tolerance schools concerning drugs and weapons. His round face held no trace of his usual friendly smile when he called a special all-school assembly. With the American flag as a background, Mr. Smiles looked taller and grimmer than his students had ever seen him.

"One strike and you're out, period," he warned. "No ifs, ands, or buts. I refuse to jeopardize the safety and education of *my students*." He paused for emphasis, cleared his throat, and raised his voice until it rang in the quiet auditorium. "We are in a war, people. A war to preserve everything that's decent and worthwhile. Today I'm going to make you a promise: As long as I am your principal, the security and well-being we enjoy here at Hillcrest High shall never be trampled on by cowardly human termites who are out to destroy what we stand for!"

Stunned silence followed his ringing announcement, followed by a loud burst of cheers and a standing ovation from the student body. If there were those in the room who sneered or disagreed, they wisely kept still and cheered with the rest.

The determined principal kept his promise. A few students tested the waters. Mr. Smiles immediately expelled them and reported the incidents to the police. No amount of pleading by parents or guardians reversed these decisions, which were fully backed by the superintendent of schools and the school board. "They knew the rules; they broke them," became a battle cry. Yet everyone at Hillcrest knew their principal felt terrible when forced to dismiss a student permanently.

The day after the lunch table discussion with Amy, Mr. Smiles called a special assembly during last period. No one seemed to know why. Juli's heart sank. What now? *Please, God,* she prayed. *We just don't need any more problems.* Her feet dragged when she slowly walked to the auditorium and sank into a seat between Dave and Shannon. "Bad news?"

Dave shrugged and looked concerned. "Maybe. Our

school hasn't done anything special or won any trophies lately." He glanced at the raised platform in front of the room and gulped. "What's your dad doing here, Shannon?"

"Are you for bein' crazy?" the Irish girl teased, then turned from Dave and faced forward. "Mercy me, it really *is* Dad!" Openmouthed, she stared while Mr. Smiles and a well-dressed Sean Riley crossed the platform from the backdrop curtains at one side. They seated themselves behind a low table that held a microphone and two gorgeous bouquets of cut flowers. Two empty chairs flanked Sean and the principal.

Juli squeezed her friend's arm. "They're smiling, so it can't be anything terrible. Mr. Smiles probably asked your dad to talk to us."

"About what?" Shannon wanted to know. "Why didn't he tell me?"

A flash of suspicion caused Juli to sit upright. She had hoped for something nice to happen. Was this it? Her suspicion grew when Mr. Smiles literally bounded to the microphone. He waited until the stragglers found seats, called the assembly to order, and burst into a wide grin.

"As you know, it gives me great pleasure when one of you does something worthy of special recognition." His smile grew until he looked like a laughing moon. "Will Shannon Riley please come forward?"

She didn't move, just gasped, "Who, me?"

"How many Shannon Rileys are in this room?" Juli demanded. "Get going!"

The next instant, paralysis set in, for Mr. Smiles beckoned and said, "You, too, Julianne."

A roar of laughter poured across the room. "Way to go, Julianne!" a mocking voice called. She felt her face redden. She'd told Mr. Smiles at least a million times to call her Juli, but he only nodded and forgot the next time he saw her.

Dave Gilmore's strong arm underneath Juli's elbow hoisted her to her feet. She grabbed Shannon's arm and pulled her up. The laughter and cheers continued during their slow progress to the platform.

"Wait 'til I get Dad home," Shannon said, half under her breath. "Look at him, grinning like the Cheddar cat. You can't tell me he didn't know about this, whatever it's for bein'."

"Cheshire, not Cheddar," Juli hissed. She kept a firm hand on Shannon's arm, not quite trusting her friend wouldn't turn and bolt out of the room.

Mr. Smiles motioned them to the empty chairs, waited until they sat down, and turned back to the student body. "First, we are happy to welcome Shannon back, after her extended absence." He tactfully omitted all mention of why she had been out of school. "Next, I want to thank Julianne Scott for being a wonderful friend and making this day possible." He turned and beamed.

Juli wanted to sink through the floor. She caught Shannon's mischievous look, now that the spotlight had turned from her to Juli.

"Mrs. Sorenson, will you please come forward and make the presentation?"

Shannon looked puzzled, but Juli's heart went into double time. She watched the honors writing teacher walk toward them. *Thank You, Lord.*

Mrs. Sorenson looked as proud as a mother hen who had somehow hatched an eagle. She took an envelope from the pocket of her well-cut blazer. "Shannon, I am thrilled to announce that your wonderful story 'Katie' has won second prize in a national teen magazine contest for high school writers." She held out the envelope. "Here is a check for $750. You will receive copies of the issue in which your story is published. Congratu—"

A storm of applause cut short the teacher's congratulations, but Shannon shook her head and looked dazed. When Mr. Smiles called for order, the Irish girl jumped up and stammered, "I—there's been a mistake." Disbelief changed to misery. "I didn't submit my story." She glanced down and bit her lip.

"That's where Julianne came in," Mr. Smiles boomed. "She knew you had the story all ready to go, so she purloined it and handed it in to Mrs. Sorenson in time for the deadline." He forced the envelope into her hands.

Purloined? My, but the principal was getting poetic! Juli felt a chuckle trying to escape. She fought to hold it back, lost the battle, and coughed loudly to disguise the laugh as best she could.

The student body went wild. Amidst the clapping, Mr.

Smiles handed each girl a bouquet. His kind eyes twinkled. "I don't know anyone who deserves these more," he said under cover of the noise. "You have both made me very proud."

"You aren't the only one." Sean Riley held out his arms. Shannon flew to them. The gratitude in Sean's face when he looked at Juli across the top of his daughter's head expressed his thanks far better than all the words in a thesaurus.

"Would you like to say a few words, Shannon?" Mr. Smiles inquired.

"No. I mean, yes, I guess so." She clutched her flowers with one hand, her acceptance letter and check in the other, and innocently said, "Th-thanks, everyone. I never dreamed I had the chance of a ghost."

"Ghost of a chance, ghost of a chance!" Juli cried, forgetting where she was. The entire group cracked up. "Rah, rah, rah; Rileyisms forever," a trio of boys chanted. Juli strongly suspected Dave, Ted, and John Foster. The final bell of the day released the girls from the howling crowd that poured out of the auditorium.

"Well, Shannon, how does it feel to be famous?" an amused voice asked from behind Juli.

She whipped around. "Dad? When did you get here?"

"Just before the presentation." His gray eyes twinkled. "My, my, but you're getting sloppy. I thought sure a first-class detective like you would see me lurking in the wings." Gary Scott pointed to one side of the curtained platform. "Congratulations, Shannon." He grasped her hand in his strong one. "You earned them. 'Katie' is a wonderful story." He laughed heartily. "You're way ahead of me! I'm beginning to think 'Murder in Black and White,' alias 'The Case of the Stuffed Skunk,' is a homing pigeon. I keep sending it out. It keeps coming back."

"Only three times," Juli loyally reminded. "Remember what we read in a writers conference newsletter? Four out of five sales of articles are made after the fifth try. But most people don't send their stories out more than four times!"

The others laughed at her earnestness, but Shannon told Dad, "Next time it will be your turn." She turned her glowing blue-gray gaze to Juli. "Or yours."

"Thanks." Juli made a face, remembering how she kept waiting for life to settle down so she could get back to her "More than Tinsel" Christmas story. She had already procrastinated until it was too late for the story to be considered for this year. A wave of determination filled her. Surely nothing more could happen to keep her from working on the plot she had so eagerly planned months earlier.

Wrong. A few hours later, John Foster and Molly Bowen showed up at the Scotts where Shannon and her father were having an impromptu celebration dinner. "Sorry to barge in like this," John apologized. "It's just that. . ." He broke off and looked at Molly.

Her warm brown eyes looked enormous and her freckles more pronounced than ever because of her white face. "We think. . .no, we're pretty sure someone has been following us."

Juli's excitement over Shannon's good news died with a thud. "Really?"

"Yeah." John shifted uneasily.

"Sit down, you two," Mom offered. "There's plenty of food."

"I don't think I can eat anything," Molly confessed. She dropped to a chair but sat on the edge and placed one hand on her stomach. "I'm all quivery."

"Same here." John also sat down.

"Have you gone to the police?" Gary Scott demanded.

The visitors shook their heads. John looked sheepish. "The first time we—"

"First time?" Dad cut in sharply. "It's happened more than once?"

Molly nodded. "Last night and today." Her voice thinned. "We thought it was a coincidence last night, but today John drove all over Bellingham."

"What kind of car was it?" Dad asked. Juli knew better than to interrupt when he was questioning someone. She sat on the edge of her chair and listened as well as she could, noticing details. How Sean Riley's hands clenched and unclenched. How big and dark Shannon's eyes looked. Were they remembering another time when someone followed *her,* with such disastrous results? Juli caught her friend's gaze and grinned reassuringly, but Shannon's answering smile looked weak.

John shook his head. "We couldn't see. Dark; a sedan

probably. The driver kept back pretty far—too far to get a license number or even a good look at the car. Sorry."

Dad wasn't through with his investigation. "Where and when did you lose whoever was tailing you?"

"A block or so before we got to my house last night," Molly said. She shuddered, then added, "We didn't really believe we were being followed. This afternoon, we did."

"We didn't go near either home today," John put in. "We headed for the nearest police precinct station as if we were going to report. The car behind took a fast right and disappeared." He grunted. "That's why we didn't tell the police. We had no proof anyone was actually following us. And of course, it could just be someone we know who's trying to give us a bad time." He looked troubled. "You don't think there's any real danger, do you? I mean, after what happened to Ted and everything. . ."

Juli felt like someone had gripped her throat with a steel hand. She held her breath and waited for Dad's answer.

"So far it doesn't appear so, but be careful," he told them. "It may be nothing. On the other hand, it's better to be too cautious than not careful enough. Keep your eyes open and let me know immediately if anything even slightly suspicious happens."

He looked around the circle at the table. "I suggest we join hands, have a prayer, then finish this delicious dinner."

Dad's matter-of-fact advice and earnest prayer brought color back into Molly's face and evidently settled her stomach. She and John ate, then excused themselves, leaving the Rileys and Scotts to speculate on the incident.

"It's so strange," Shannon said. "It doesn't make sense."

A familiar twang of nerves caused Juli to say, "Exactly what we thought when Ted was hurt. Right?"

Shannon agreed. "And when someone slashed the tires on Amy's car." She laughed nervously. "So what do Amy and Ted, John and Molly have in common?"

Juli grabbed onto the idea with both hands. "Lots. For starters, they're all sophomores. They're all members of the church youth group, too."

"Along with a bundle of other things," Shannon chimed in. "Ted and Amy are twins, but John is only one of Amy's ex-boyfriends. Besides, where does that leave Molly? She and John have only been good friends for a few months."

After the others had gone, Juli curled up on her bed with Clue and her journal. She wrote,

God, we have to be overlooking something. Is there a reason behind all this? Everyone involved so far has some kind of ties with the Hiltons. Does someone have a vendetta against the family? If so, why? They are ordinary people living ordinary lives.

Juli stopped to read what she had written. Her pencil idly moved from word to word. When she came to "so far," she paused. A chill chased up her spine. Why had she included that? Was concern about her friends coloring her judgment and making her afraid of what else might happen? If something did, to whom? Even more important, why? Neither Clue nor the journal had answers. Juli put down her pencil, said her prayers, and fell asleep. What an up-and-down day! Maybe tomorrow would even out.

So much for Juli's high hopes. Shannon walked on air with Juli feeling nearly as fine, but the day turned ghastly with the evening news. Another robbery had occurred, this time in one of the branches of the bank where Sean Riley worked.

CHAPTER 11

"Just when things are looking good, bam!—more trouble," Juli complained to Shannon on the bus the next morning. "I'm beginning to feel like a yo-yo."

"Same here." Shannon gave a furtive glance over her shoulder and leaned closer to Juli. "It was bad enough just seeing the afterwards of a bank robbery. This time it could have been *Dad's* bank. It's so scary."

"I know." Juli didn't have the heart to tell her friend she meant "aftermath," not "afterwards." She stared out the window at drizzling rain. "The weather doesn't help. Or the fact this robbery was exactly like the one at the Chuckanut Community Bank." Juli began counting off on her fingers. "One, late afternoon. Two, a single male figure. Three, a ski cap pulled low, and a denim jacket with the collar turned up. Four, the robber approached the teller, pulled a gun, and slid a note to her. The note demanded bills from the cash drawer and warned her to say nothing for at least ten minutes. Five, a skull and crossbones instead of a signature."

"There was one difference this time, though," Shannon grimly reminded. "The teller was so nervous she fainted after handing over the bills."

"Right." Juli absentmindedly clasped and unclasped her hands. "According to the news, the last thing the teller remembered was hearing a click and thinking the robber had cocked his gun." Fear scurried through her.

Shannon's eyes turned gray with horror. "He might actually have shot her?"

Juli checked to make sure no one could hear. "Dad says it's hard to tell. When robbers get too confident, they sometimes get careless. They may also turn violent if things don't go exactly as planned." She idly traced circles on the back of her hand with a forefinger. "I just wish they'd catch the creep."

"You aren't the only one," Shannon agreed.

The lunch bunch who gathered in the cafeteria at noon felt the same. Their conversation centered on the robbery and the mysterious car and driver who had tailed John and Molly. Brett Jones grew angry. "Why don't the police do something?" he snapped. "It's outrageous for a neat city like Bellingham to have to put up with this kind of thing."

Juli started to defend the police department, but Shannon shuddered and pleaded, "Please, can we talk about something else? I'm sick of crime."

Brett did a complete about-face and turned on the

charm. "Sorry. What's happening with the Adopt-a-Grandparent program? I haven't been able to do any visiting yet but I know some of you have. How's it going?"

"Good," everyone except Amy chorused. She said, "The only visiting I've been doing is with Ted." She stared at the table. "I–I never knew how much I cared about him until now." Huddled in an oversized white shirt, she looked small and vulnerable. Her everyone-look-at-me attitude that irritated others had at least temporarily disappeared.

Juli's naturally warm heart opened to her. "Ted's doing fine, isn't he, Amy?"

"Yes. He's home now. You can come see him whenever."

"Just what we've been waiting to hear," Dave put in. Shannon only smiled, but happiness gleamed in her eyes.

"Good," Brett said. "About the Adopt-a-Grandparent program?"

Juli beamed. She wouldn't have believed a cool senior like Brett Jones would be interested in older people. He was the kind of boy people associated with Homecoming and Prom King. "It really is great. Reports are coming in from both visitors and, uh, . . .visitees?" The group howled at her new word.

"Who are you visiting?" Brett wanted to know.

Juli bit her tongue. With Amy caught up in her own problems and Ted hurt, how could she tell the group whose name she had drawn? It had been shock enough when she opened the small slip of paper and read:

"My grandson comes often, but I don't get to see enough of my granddaughter. I guess she is too busy with school and church activities. I'm not blaming her. As people say, you're only young once. But you're only old once, too. I get lonely. If a nice girl would stop by now and then, I'd appreciate it so much."

The note had been signed by Amy's grandmother.

Now Juli only said, "I'm visiting a really nice lady." She impulsively asked, "Amy, since Ted is home, would you go with me? I'd love to have you. My lady would, too."

Genuine pleasure sparkled in the small blond's face. "Sure. When?"

Juli remembered how Shannon always said that in spite of Amy's irritating superiority, sometimes she felt a lonely little girl lived inside the cheerleader. A girl who had to keep winning honors to prove her value to the world and herself.

"Tomorrow right after school, if you're free."

Shannon grinned. "I'll be happy to drop in on Ted if you want to go, Amy."

"Thanks. He's ready to climb the walls," Amy told her. "We can take my car, Juli. It has all new tires."

For the rest of the day Juli alternated between wanting to warn Amy about who they were visiting, and having cold feet about the whole thing. What if the other girl grew so angry she refused to go? The last few days had begun an uneasy healing between them, and Juli hated to have anything rock the boat.

Somehow, thinking about her relationship with Amy brought a certain dark-haired senior to mind. Her heartbeat quickened. She hadn't decided if she even liked Brett very well, although his interest in the Adopt-a-Grandparent program made her feel warmer toward him. On the other hand, innocently or otherwise, he was a source of trouble. Amy had claimed Brett as her personal property. He seemed to go along with it. Yet it didn't stop him from paying attention to Juli, Shannon, even to Molly, who just grinned and raised a skeptical reddish eyebrow at his flirting.

Dave resented Brett. It showed more in what he didn't say or do than what he did. It showed in the way he had frozen at Juli's locker after school that day. Brett had walked her there. Dave grew all rigid and disapproving when Brett nodded at him, smiled his Hollywood smile at Juli, and said, "Thanks. It's a date."

"You have a date with Jones?" Dave asked in a stunned voice after Brett sauntered down the hall, carelessly waved, and disappeared around a corner.

Juli felt herself turn scarlet. Why should she feel guilty, as if she'd been caught shoplifting or cheating on a test? "Not really. I mean, it's not a *date* date. He needed a copy of *A Tale of Two Cities* and asked if he could borrow mine." She jerked open her locker door, glad that some of the stuff inside fell out. Kneeling to pick it up meant a chance to hide her face from Dave, who had turned ominously quiet and didn't bend down to help her pick up the mess.

"Funny," he finally said in a flat voice. "I'd think the library would have at least one copy available of a book as well-known as that one."

Juli scrambled to her feet, angry that the sight of Brett made her heart bounce; and angry at Dave for just standing there with arms folded and steady blue gaze fixed on her telltale face. "Am I on trial here? You're standing there like a judge who has already tried, convicted, and sentenced me!"

Dave broke into unexpected laughter. His blue eyes twinkled. "Right. That's why I'm driving you home, to see that you don't break parole."

"You are impossible." But Juli's ready sense of humor betrayed her. She couldn't help laughing when Dave cocked his head and grinned his maddening grin. "I give up, warden. Let's go."

He loosely draped one arm over her shoulders. "Does Madame Prisoner have time for a soft drink before her date that isn't shows up for the book?"

"She does." Juli's world brightened. Brett might be attractive, but losing Dave's friendship was something she didn't even want to consider.

Evidently Dave's mind ran double track with hers. On the way home he said, "I know your being my girlfriend *pro tem* doesn't give me a right to tell you who you can go out with, Juli. It's just that Brett Jones is so, uh. . .don't you think he's kind of phony? It's not because I'm jealous." He glanced at her and the corners of his mouth turned down.

"Okay, so I'm a little jealous." He hesitated. "I guess I'm under-impressed with good-looking guys who drive cool cars and turn on the charm every time a girl walks by."

His evaluation strengthened Juli's doubts, but she didn't give him the satisfaction of agreeing. Dave didn't seem to notice. He added, "Guys like that also can cause trouble between girls, especially when one of the girls is Amy."

"I know." It slipped out on its own. "Ted and John don't act too crazy about Brett either."

"They aren't." A certain reserve in Dave's voice carried over to his next words. "I guess no one who shows up out of the blue and comes on like Superman would be all that well accepted." He shrugged. "How come you asked Amy to go visiting with you?"

Loyalty locked Juli's tongue. "It will be good for her. Me, too."

" 'Me, too'? Bad grammar, Miss Author-to-be. Speaking of authors, isn't it great about Shannon? What's she going to do with the prize money?"

Juli heaved a secret sigh of relief. She hated keeping things from Dave, but Amy would never forgive her if she told her real reason for taking the other girl visiting. A ripple of laughter chased away problems. "Do you want it in her own words, or translated?"

Dave groaned. "I feel a Rileyism coming on. Give it to me straight."

Juli choked out between bouts of laughter, "You asked

for it; here it is. Ta da." She dropped into a reasonable imitation of Shannon's brogue. " 'I'm for puttin' it away in the auld stocking so when we be for flyin' the henhouse, maybe to Ireland, 'twill be there waitin' for us.' "

Dave looked totally astounded. "You're kidding!"

"I am not," Juli defended herself, wiping tears from her eyes. "It took even me a few moments to figure out Shannon meant putting her prize money in the bank, the equivalent of the old sock people used to use. Her flying the henhouse means flying the coop, of course." She burst into giggles, with Dave joining in.

Neither Juli nor any of her lunch bunch was laughing the next day. Brett made his few-minute stop at the Scotts to pick up *A Tale of Two Cities* sound like a prom date. Amy looked hurt and turned sulky. Dave exchanged knowing glances with the other boys and shot Juli an *I-told-you-so* look. Shannon and Molly didn't crack a smile and started talking about something else as soon as possible.

Juli felt a lump of anger form inside her. Even if Brett's visit had been a real date, he should know better than to make a big deal out of it in front of another girl who obviously liked him. His dark good looks might attract, but when it came to the consideration department, he scored a big fat zero.

Juli dreaded meeting Amy after school, but didn't know how to get out of it. With a quick prayer for help, she slowly walked to the red Mustang and slid in.

Amy put the key in the ignition and said tonelessly, "Which way?"

Juli swallowed. She took out the creased slip of paper she'd put in her backpack that morning. "Before we go, I need to level with you," she began.

"If it's about Brett Jones, I don't want to hear it." Amy tossed her head but the stricken look in her eyes showed she cared more than she would admit.

"It isn't, but while we're talking about him, you may as well know he's nothing to me," Juli blurted. "Brett's tall, good-looking, and all that, but TDSC just isn't Dave Gilmore." Relief washed through Juli. She hadn't realized the mental comparisons she'd been making since Brett first showed up at church. Putting her feelings into words made her see how much she actually believed them.

"TDSC?" Amy sounded relieved, but still suspicious.

"Shannon and I made it up. It stands for tall, dark, and super cool," Juli admitted.

The blond girl giggled and thawed. "Bingo. You're right, though. Brett isn't Dave Gilmore." Before amazement at Amy's candid agreement sank in, she added, "As long as Dave seems perfectly happy hanging out with you, I'll just have to settle for Brett." Some of her perkiness returned. "Okay with you?"

Juli knew better than to commit herself. Amy had a way of repeating conversations, sometimes maliciously. She also reported her interpretations and they didn't always match what was actually said. "Now that we've settled

Brett Jones's future, I have a confession." Juli unfolded the paper and handed it to Amy, silently praying the other girl would be able to accept its contents.

A delicate blush colored Amy's face when she read the first sentence. It deepened to scorching red when she went on. To Juli's surprise, shame and deep unhappiness showed in the smaller girl's light blue eyes when she looked up. "I'm sorry. I never dreamed Grandma felt like this." A flood drenched the long, darkened eyelashes. "Juli, when you went to see her, did she say anything? About me, I mean?" Amy dabbed at her eyes with a tissue.

"She only said how proud she is of all your accomplishments," Juli quietly said. "You're so lucky to have a grandmother. In my family, it's just Mom, Dad and me. Not that I'm complaining. They're great."

"I know." Amy's voice sounded muffled. "You don't even argue, do you?"

"Are you kidding? I'm a teenager, right?" Juli laughed, then quickly sobered. "We disagree, but we don't argue much. Especially since losing Dad for what felt like a lifetime." She cleared her throat. "Mop up, will you? We're off to Grandmother's house!"

Amy's apology to her grandmother raised Juli's opinion of her considerably, and led to a great visit. That opinion skyrocketed the next day when Amy frankly told what happened. Juli knew a whole lot more prayers than her own frantic one were being answered in unexpected ways.

Life's yo-yo hadn't finished with Juli, her family, and

friends. Several alarming events occurred so close together they left little time to stop reeling from one before the next happened. Dave found scratches around the keyhole on the driver's door of his Mustang. Strange footprints showed up in the rain-softened flower bed beneath the Rileys' front window. Someone dropped a note made of words cut from a newspaper through the mail slot of Juli's front door. It warned: YOU'LL PAY FOR WHAT YOU DID.

"Great," she told Mom and Dad. "All I have to do is figure out what I did." She stared at the note. "I haven't killed anyone. I haven't even attacked anyone. Hey, wait a minute." Excitement flooded Juli's body. "The rottweiler." Her voice rose to a high pitch. "The owner must have written this. He was angry enough to massacre me." She licked dry lips. "Now it looks like he may."

Gary Scott's eyes flashed. "Over my dead body," he promised.

Juli shuddered. "Thanks, Dad, but please, can't you put it a different way?"

CHAPTER 12

A little over an hour later, Gary Scott and Juli rang the doorbell of a modest home not far from the scene of the girl-dog-bicycle collision. Finding Bruno and his owner had been fairly simple. The Scotts retraced Juli and Shannon's route and asked people in the area who had a rottweiler. Now, familiar and furious barking showed they had the right place. So did a shouted, "Quiet, Bruno," just before someone flung open the front door.

Juli clenched sweaty fingers. The same man who had roared at her, and the same rottweiler she'd crashed into, stood behind the frail protection of a screen door. In spite of Juli's anger at the cheap and cowardly way of taking revenge—the anonymous note—the fear she had felt the day of the accident surged through her.

"Well, for the love of Mike, look who's here." The dog owner threw aside the screen door and stepped out. Bruno followed, rumbling low in his throat. To Juli and her Dad's utter amazement, the man beamed as though Juli were a long-lost daughter. He exclaimed, "Am I ever glad to see you!"

Caught totally off guard, she stammered, "You–you are?"

"Yeah." He looked sheepish and glanced from her to Dad. "Sorry I blew my top that day. It's a bad habit. I yell first, simmer down later. You weren't really hurt, were you? My wife gave me what for when I got home." He rolled his eyes. "Uh, Bruno and I tried to find you but nobody around here knew who you were."

All Juli's suspicion fled. The regret in his eyes reflected honesty apology. "We don't live near here. My friend and I were just out for a bike ride. Anyway, I was only shaken and skinned up. It's all right." She smiled.

"Thanks!" A heartfelt sigh escaped. "No excuse for me, except I'm a little nutty over Bruno. We got him when he was a pup. Never had kids. I guess we're too protective. Say, can I offer you anything? A soda, maybe?"

"Thanks, but no." Gary Scott shook hands with the man, but acted funny.

Juli wondered. She didn't say anything until they started walking toward home, then she asked, "Dad, how come you acted so eager to get away?"

"Good detective work, Watson. I was."

"Why, Sherlock?" Juli stopped short, ignoring the fact they had a long way to go and needed to keep moving if they were going to make it home before dark.

"Can't you guess?" he teased. A twinkle in his gray eyes challenged her.

Juli thought about it. "I don't know. Oh! If we'd stuck around, the man would have started asking questions about why we looked him up. We don't have a good excuse, since we aren't suing him or claiming damages. Right?" The upward quirk of Dad's lips told her she was getting warmer. She increased her pace to match his long stride. "After the guy acted so happy to see us, no way could we say we came to confront him about sending me an anonymous letter!"

"You said 'acted' happy to see us. Do you think he was acting?"

"You must be kidding." Juli laughed. "I suspect Bruno's owner is exactly what he said—a person who loses his cool, bellows at anyone around, and feels ashamed of himself when he has time to think things over."

"Go to the head of the class," Dad said approvingly. "Keep up your insight into human nature, Juli, and you'll make one great mystery writer. Yes!" He made fists of his hands and shot his arms up toward the rainwashed sky.

His compliment made Juli feel good from the top of her head to the bare toes in her sandals. "Thanks, Dad." A breeze off the bay tickled her arms below her purple tee shirt sleeves and sent a chill through her. "I kind of wish he'd been guilty. Now we don't know who sent the letter, or why."

"Tomorrow's the last day of school, isn't it? What

time do you get out?"

"There's an assembly, we turn in books, clean out our lockers, that kind of stuff. No lunch. We'll be through before noon."

"Good. I want you to bring all the kids in what you call your 'lunch bunch' home with you, or at least as many as can make it. In the past few weeks, all of you have been threatened, or had something suspicious happen. Try not to scare your friends, but tell them it's important for us to take a long, hard look. We need to see if there's some kind of pattern forming here."

"What about Brett Jones?" Juli asked. "He's been hanging out with us but nothing funny has happened to him. At least I don't think so. Actually, he's sort of a private person. He doesn't say much about his folks."

Dad speeded up. "Could be a messy divorce, or fighting in the home. A lot of kids don't want others to know their personal problems. It doesn't appear Brett is involved, so you can use your own judgment about including him."

The decision was swept out of Juli's hands in a bizarre turn of events. The minute she and Shannon stepped from the bus the next morning, Brett, Amy, Dave, John, and Molly were waiting. Their unusually serious faces showed they had news. Juli took a deep breath. "What?"

"Someone left me a not-so-filled-with-love note last night," Brett reported. "I found it under my windshield wiper this morning." He held up a paper.

Juli felt her knees turn rubbery. Her mouth dried. *The message had been formed from words and letters cut from a newspaper.* It read: KNOCK IT OFF OR TAKE THE CONSEQUENCES.

"Hey, are you okay?" Dave demanded when Juli took a step backward and stumbled. A strong arm shot out and kept her from falling.

She felt her eyes burn. "No. Brett, everyone, somebody sent me a threatening message too." Juli gulped. "It was made the same way as yours."

"Why didn't you tell me?" Shannon cried.

"Dad said not to discuss it until he has the chance to talk with all of us. He wants you to come to our place as soon as school gets out today. Ted, too."

"No problem." Amy looked frightened, but determined. "Your dad has the right idea. Every one of us is a target, but why?" She wrapped her arms around her slim body, even though June sun poured down on the group from a cloudless sky. "What did any of us do to deserve this?"

No one had an answer, either then or at the impromptu meeting held at the Scotts' that afternoon. Gary Scott quietly but painstakingly pumped every person present for the smallest detail. He made notes about their schedules, where they had been, when, and with whom. Suddenly he straightened to military erectness. "The day of the robbery at Chuckanut Community Bank, you were at the Pizza Palace. Were any other members of your church youth group with you?"

"No," they chorused. "Most of the kids had other things to do that day."

"Next question. What about other times and place where all of you were present?" He grinned. "I don't mean at church, school, or in the cafeteria."

They couldn't think of any.

"Is there something weird about that Wednesday?" Shannon asked.

Gary Scott shrugged. "Who knows?" He turned a direct gray gaze on Brett. "If I heard right, you weren't at the Pizza Palace with the others."

Brett looked regretful. "Sorry I can't be of more help." He laughed. "I had to ask what the Pizza Palace was!" He glanced around the circle of friends. "Remember the first week I came to Sunday school? Amy mentioned it because she saw a white Mustang in the parking lot that looked like mine but wasn't."

"So much for that clue. If you weren't with the others, there appears to be no reason for you to be targeted," Dad remarked.

"I do hang out with them." Brett glanced from person to person and let his gaze stop at Juli. "Mr. Scott, this is a pretty special bunch of kids. Going to church and getting to know them has really made a difference in my life."

Once more Juli forgave Brett his weaknesses. Anyone who sounded that sincere couldn't be totally shallow. To her disappointment, Dad didn't continue with the discussion. He just said, "Thanks for coming. Be sure to report anything out of the ordinary, no matter how small. Okay?"

"Sure." The lunch bunch said good-bye and left. Only Dave and Shannon remained. Gary Scott had unobtrusively told Juli to have them stay. Something in his voice warned he had a reason. Juli whispered his request to her friends and the three of them waved off the others.

"I do have a reason," Dad admitted to the three teens when they were alone. "At this point I don't want to make a big deal of it, but you all are clear thinkers and not apt to panic. So is Ted, broken leg and all, and John. I don't know Brett or Molly that well. Amy is Amy." He grinned. "Anyway, the more people in on a secret, the more chance there is of a leak."

"You really do suspect something, don't you, Dad?" Juli leaned forward from her place on the couch between Shannon and Dave.

"Enough to ask Andrew and Mary Payne to drop by. They'll be here soon."

A thrill went through Juli. She heard Shannon gasp, felt Dave straighten as if stung by an angry hornet. "You're calling in the FBI? Because of us?"

"Not officially. I'm on leave, remember? I just want them to be aware we may have witnesses to a crime."

"Witnesses!" Juli exploded off the couch. "Us? No way. The bank robbery was over and the thief long gone before we ever came out of the Pizza Palace."

"You know that and I know that. Someone else may not," Dad quietly said.

Dave and Shannon also leaped up. "How could we see something and not know we saw something?" Shannon cried.

The doorbell rang before Gary Scott could answer. "Sit down," he told the excited teens. "I'll let Andrew and Mary explain."

"Someone had better," Dave muttered. "I guess if anyone can, it will be the Paynes." He grinned. "Every time I see those two I remember how we suspected *them* of being crooks at Skagit House. We sure were wrong."

Juli only nodded and greeted brick-haired Andrew Payne and his attractive wife, Mary. Neither resembled stereotypes of an FBI agent, but when the occasion demanded, they were masters of disguise. The Paynes had become warm friends with Juli's family and friends after Scott and Gilmore's first case, "Mysterious Monday," was solved.

Andrew's likable grin changed to a pretend scowl. "Why am I not surprised to learn you three are involved in another mystery? Let's have it."

"It isn't just us this time, sir." Dave spread his hands out. "So are Ted and Amy Hilton and John Foster. Also Molly Bowen and Brett Jones."

Andrew wasted no time or words. "Who are the last two? I know the others."

"Molly's a sophomore girl John likes. Brett's a senior who transferred to Hillcrest just a few weeks ago," Juli dutifully reported.

"Funny thing to do with so little time before graduation." Andrew grunted. "What's he like?"

Juli stared at her fingers, glad when Shannon piped up, "Tall, dark, super cool." She giggled. "He acts like God created him as a gift to women."

"Excuse me?" Andrew's jaw dropped.

Juli groaned. "She means Brett thinks he's God's gift to women. Remember Shannon's Rileyisms?"

"Oh, yeah." Andrew ran one hand across his chin. He evidently hadn't shaved since morning, for the slight stubble rasped and set Juli's nerves on edge. "So what else do you know about Jones? How's he involved?"

"Someone's after him, too." Juli wanted to move away from the subject of Brett Jones's good looks before Dave aired his opinions. "Brett found a note under his windshield wiper. It looked like the one I received, except his said, 'KNOCK IT OFF OR TAKE THE CONSEQUENCES.' "

"Get your note, will you please, Juli?" Mary put in. She and Andrew examined it thoroughly for a long time. They also asked the teens to repeat everything they could remember about the day at the Pizza Palace. When Juli felt as if she'd been turned inside out or examined with an X-ray machine, Andrew fitted the fingers of one hand against the other.

"Gary may be right," he announced. "If someone believes any or all of you witnessed something the day of the robbery, it doesn't matter how innocent you are. What's important is that someone may feel threatened.

Not by what you saw but by what he *thinks* you may have seen." His eyes half closed and he stared at the ceiling. "How crowded was this pizza joint?"

"Packed. It took forever to get served," Shannon said, her eyes wide.

"People coming in and out in crowds? All ages?"

"Yeah." Dave crossed and uncrossed his long legs. "Lots and lots of them."

The pupils of Andrew's eyes turned to shiny steel drills. "Then what's to prevent the robber from removing his cap and gloves, turning down the collar of his jacket, and blending in with the rest of the hungry horde? I assume he isn't the only teenager in Bellingham who has a denim jacket."

"I don't know anyone who doesn't own one," Shannon whispered.

Juli's stomach felt the way it had once when she pushed the DOWN button of a superfast elevator on a visit to one of Seattle's tall buildings.

"Just what I was thinking," Gary Scott tossed in. "What safer place for him? Who would suspect a robber of hanging around? Logically, they would split."

Juli's mind leaped ahead. "When the police came, the bank robber could rush out with the rest of us and act shocked." She slumped back against the couch.

"Let's go over it once more," Andrew ordered. "No one is suppressing evidence, but sometimes knowing there's a real need to remember helps. Close your eyes. Pretend to be in the Pizza Palace. Use your five senses. Remember: Sights, sounds, smells, touch, and taste can help trigger memories."

They obeyed. Dave sniffed. "I smell pizza. It's making me hungry."

"I can see how crowded the tables are," Shannon said.

"I taste warm pizza and ice water." Something teased at Juli's mind. Her hand tingled. "I feel ice water, too. We used it to help mop up Amy after the spill."

Andrew attacked like a hawk on a newly hatched chick. "Spill? What spill?"

Juli's eyes popped open. "A boy jostled Amy's arm and she dropped pizza on Ted's letter jacket. We tried to clean it up. He was furious."

"I assume the name of your school was on Ted's jacket?" Andrew asked.

Juli stared at the FBI agent without really seeing him. "Yes, but—of course! If the robber was actually there, he'd know where to find us!"

"Especially if that robber was the boy who bumped into Amy," Dad said. "Did any of you see the person? Did he speak?"

"Ted told him to watch where he was going. The guy said he was sorry. The rest of us were too busy with Amy to pay attention." Shannon's fingers bit into Juli's arm. "Now Ted has a broken leg from a hit-and-run accident." Every trace of color drained from her face. "Maybe it wasn't an accident after all."

CHAPTER 13

The persecution of Juli and her friends ended as suddenly as it began. After the rash of incidents, nothing happened for several days. Was the freedom permanent, or only an interlude before something worse happened?

"I feel like we're walking over the thin crust of a volcano," Juli told Shannon one lazy afternoon on the Scotts' deck. Armed with a pitcher of icy lemonade, they had settled down and prepared to enjoy being out of school for the summer.

The girls couldn't have chosen a more perfect place. Beauty surrounded them, from a multitude of singing birds to heavily laden fruit trees that promised a good harvest. Well-tended flower beds and a vegetable garden added charm. The variety of large trees and shrubs muted traffic from the street in front of the house. The backyard offered an ideal spot for sharing confidences.

Juli watched a tiny hummingbird at a nearby feeder.

Its beating wings reminded her of herself at times, and of something she'd been wanting to discuss with Shannon. "Dr. Marlowe says Dad is okay to go back to work. He's at local headquarters right now." In a burst of honesty she added, "I *never* want him to go back to the State Patrol! After what happened, I don't think I can handle it." She traced a pattern on the frosty surface of her glass.

"I keep praying and praying Dad's story will sell so he can stay home and write. It isn't happening. He's getting discouraged because 'Murder in Black and White' keeps coming back. By the way, he dumped the subtitle. One editor said adding 'alias The Case of the Stuffed Skunk' was too light for the story."

She fell silent, so silent a bright-eyed gray squirrel peered from the leafy branches of a maple tree. He whisked down the rough trunk and ran across the smooth green grass to a lofty fir. Juli went on, knowing Shannon was equally interested in Dad and his budding writing career. "The other day he said he didn't think he'd send his story out again."

She deepened her voice to a reasonable imitation of Gary Scott's and quoted, " 'I know the fact editors are scribbling encouraging personal notes to me means a lot, but you can't pay bills with them.' " Juli grinned mischievously. "Dad doesn't know it, but I sent his story out the very next day. Mrs. Sorenson just can't be wrong about how good it is."

"Of course she can't!" Shannon agreed. The next second, her Irish blue eyes turned gray. "Have you told your dad how you feel? About his job, I mean?"

A ray of hope penetrated Juli's gloom. Her spirits quickly sank. "How can I? It has to be his decision. Even Mom says so."

Shannon lapsed into the Irish brogue that crept into her speech during times of stress or deep feeling. "She may know best, and I'm not for goin' contrary to Mom's advice," she softly said. "Yet if 'twere me, I'd be for knowin' my father needed to be told how I felt. Don't you think your dad's the same?"

"Maybe." Hope fluttered butterfly wings, then stilled. "How can I ever put it into words?" A rush of emotion surged through her. "I'm afraid I'll start bawling before I get halfway through, or not make any sense."

Shannon gave her a quick hug. "Use the talents God gave you. Write your dad a letter. That way you can take as much time as you need. He will also have time to really consider what you say before you talk."

The butterfly quivered again. "I do come out a lot better on paper, don't I?"

Shannon smiled. "Sometimes." She leaned her head back against the brightly patterned chaise lounge. Sunlight dappled her expressive face. "Aren't you glad we're friends?" she irrelevantly asked. "I can't imagine life in Bellingham without you." She turned to face Juli. "Remember when we promised to always be friends?" A cloud sneaked in front of the sun for a few seconds. It cast a shadow on Shannon's face. "We've gone through a lot together."

"I know." Yet Juli's attention had been diverted. The idea of writing Dad a letter had never occurred to her. Once Shannon mentioned it, it seemed the most natural way in the world to tell Dad how she felt.

Shannon had an uncanny way of sensing Juli's moods. Now she smiled at her friend. "Why don't you go write your letter? I can see it coming on." She yawned. "I'm too comfortable to get up and go home. Besides, it's perfect here. I can let down and relax." She yawned again and stretched her muscles.

Juli started to get up, her mind racing with sentences and phrases. "Are you sure you're okay? It doesn't seem very polite to invite you over then take off."

"Oh, if you refill my lemonade glass before you begin your masterpiece, all will be forgiven." Juli obligingly poured and her friend drank it down. "Mmmm. Good." She handed Juli her glass and yawned for the third time. "We've been going on for so long, this is a good time to crash. Wake me up when you get your letter written. Now, scat!" Shannon made a shooing motion.

"I think you mean 'on the go,' not 'going on,' " Juli told her.

"Whatever." Shannon airily waved one hand before closing her eyes.

Juli laughed and headed for her room. It would go faster on the computer, but the feel of a pencil or pen in her hand sometimes helped her think more clearly. As she sat, she glanced at Clue in his usual place on her desk. The stuffed bear's shiny dark eyes and soft plush body were as much a part of Juli's writing as the freshly sharpened pencil and clean white pages of a new notebook.

She made several false starts, crossed them out, then dropped her pad and pencil to bury her face in her arms. "Please, God, help me say what I feel." A long and quiet time later, Juli picked up the pencil and began to write. When she finished, instead of rereading it as she usually would, she folded the letter and put it in an envelope. Her feelings had poured from her heart through the pencil and onto the now full page. Juli knew if she read it over, she might have second thoughts and never give it to Dad.

"Not that it matters," she told Clue. "If I live to be older than Mount Baker, I'll probably still remember what I said. I wonder how Dad will feel?"

She asked Shannon the same question when she reached the patio and found her friend wide awake and watching Mr. Squirrel frisk between trees. "I told it like it is," Juli confessed.

"Whether he agrees or not, your dad will respect you and your right to say what you think," Shannon comforted.

"I know. He always has. So has Mom," Juli told her. *Oh yeah?* an unwelcome inner voice nagged. *Then how come you're as nervous as a long-tailed cat in a roomful of rocking chairs?* All the justification Juli could muster about the whole family's future being at stake couldn't drown the sneering little voice.

After dinner and dishes, Juli handed Dad the letter. "I

wrote this for you today. If–if you want to talk after you read it, I'll be on the patio."

"For me?" Dad looked surprised. "Mom too?"

"Uh, yeah. Maybe you want to read it out loud to her." An obstruction rose in Juli's throat. She bolted outside, left the patio door ajar so she could hear, and perched on the edge of a nearby deck chair.

"Gary, is something bothering Juli?" the eavesdropper heard Mom ask.

"It sounds like it." Dad's grave voice brought a rush of tears to Juli's eyes. She heard the rustle of paper, then stillness before he began reading words she knew only too well. Shame scorched her. Why hadn't she just talked with her parents? What had felt so right when she put it on paper now seemed stupid and condemning. Had she run ahead of God again, instead of making sure she was doing what He'd want her to do in this situation? She cringed as Dad's voice began.

> *Dear Dad,*
>
> *I'm afraid I'll bawl like a little kid if I try and tell you how I feel. I probably wouldn't even have had the courage to write this if Shannon hadn't said you'd want to know how I feel. I've always been proud you had a job where you could help people, but I'm scared to death for you to go back on patrol. It doesn't matter how much I pray about it. Every time I remember the night*

you didn't come home, I feel sick inside.

I know you have to make the decision that's right for you. I wish I could promise to accept it and not be scared anymore. Is there some way for you to help me get over my fear? Just the thought of you being late on a winter night leaves me shaking.

When I was a little kid, I could always climb into your lap and know everything would be all right. Now that I'm trying to grow up, it isn't that easy. I've learned even Christian families don't always get to live happily ever after, like in the storybooks.

I love you, Dad. Thanks for listening.

Juli crossed her arms over her chest and huddled into a ball of misery. Weren't Dad and Mom ever going to say anything? An eternity of waiting later, she heard slow steps coming toward her. The patio door were flung wide open. Strong arms picked her up and carried her inside. Dad laid her on the couch, knelt beside it, and took both of her hands in his. Juli felt she'd gone back ten years. She clung to him, feeling nothing on earth could hurt any of them.

"I am so sorry," Gary Scott said in a choky voice. "I should have told you sooner, but I wanted it to be a surprise. I *am* going back to work, Juli, but not as a patrol officer. A desk job recently opened up. After a lot of prayer and discussing things with your mother, I put in for it.

Confirmation came through today. I'll be working inside, not on the streets and highways."

Juli could barely believe her own ears. "You will?" She stared into her father's face, noting the compassion in his quiet gray eyes. Suspicion formed. "Did you know how I felt? How Mom felt?"

"More than you'll ever realize. You've been good sports. You've supported me in doing what I honestly believed God wanted." A poignant expression came across his face. "Now I feel I'm supposed to move on." He shifted position and squeezed her hands tightly. "I'm proud of you for writing the letter, Juli. I know it took a whole lot of courage."

"You don't think it's dumb?"

"Dumb?" He stared at his daughter, then threw his head back and laughed. "Anything but!" A teasing light crept into his eyes. "Julianne Scott, this is some of the finest writing you have ever done. I suggest you tuck it away. If you ever need to show pathos in a story, you'll have an excellent example."

"Thanks, Dad." She freed his hands. "Excuse me, but I have to call Shannon."

"Why am I not surprised?" Dad threw his hands into the air in mock dismay. "Seems like I've heard that line before." He chuckled. When Juli came back from making her call, Gary Scott demanded, "So, what did she say?" He laughed again. "More important, how did she say it?"

Juli felt lighter than air. She giggled. "Shannon smugly

announced, and I quote, 'All's swell that ends swell.' Isn't that just like her?" Juli threw her arms around Dad, then sternly turned to her mother. "How could you keep his secret?"

Anne Scott grinned until she looked more like her daughter than ever. "I don't tell all I know, even to Dad." She ignored his surprised glance. "For instance, I've also come to a career decision." She cleared her throat. "Attention, please. This first-grade teacher has just finished making arrangements for next year."

"What kind of arrangements?" Juli held her breath. Mom liked teaching, but her only daughter still didn't like the prospect of having to come home to an empty house day after day.

Anne smirked and looked as smug as Shannon had sounded. "Pardon me if I boast, but I intend to have the best of both worlds. I discovered another teacher who likes homemaking as much as I do. We both also like teaching. So, we talked with the building principal. *Voilá!*" Happiness widened her smile. "We're going to team teach next year. I'll take mornings; she wants afternoons. It's a real answer to prayer."

Dad grabbed her and waltzed her around the room. "This calls for a celebration," he declared. "Beat the drums. Sound the cymbals. Translated, that means, call Sean and Shannon, Juli. We'll do an ice cream run."

"Dad and I never turn down an invitation to Thirty-Some Flavors," Shannon remarked when she and her father reached the Scott home.

Everyone howled, but when Juli corrected, "Thirty-One, not Thirty-Some," Shannon stuck her nose in the air. She further declared it wasn't her fault the "ice creamery" didn't know what to name itself, even if it did have great treats.

An exciting answering machine message awaited the two families when they returned to Juli's home. Dave Gilmore wanted to know whether Gary and Anne Scott were available to chaperone a one-day youth group hiking trip to Mount Baker the coming Saturday. Although, as he put it, they'd really be hiking on Mount Shuksan. "Kareem and Jasmine Thompson said they could probably trust your folks to help them chaperone," he teased when Juli returned his call. "Mr. Riley's welcome, too, if he's available."

The Scotts agreed, but Sean regretfully said, "Sorry. The bank officers are on edge. We're beefing up security and doing training on how to handle emergency situations. We're also preparing for the end of the fiscal year. You'll have to count me out this time." He smiled at his daughter. "Shannon's welcome to go."

A ways and means meeting followed the next day. So many of the group wanted to go on the trip, Kareem decided to take the church bus instead of private vehicles. "Seven o'clock sharp at the church parking lot," he told them.

Brett Jones shook his head. "I can't leave until ten, but that's no problem. I'll drive up." He looked straight at

Juli and said, "I'd be glad for company, if someone would consider waiting and going with me. . ."

Dave stiffened and glared, but Amy slid into the opening like roasted clams into melted butter. "That's great, Brett! Thanks for remembering I hate to get up early. Ten will be fine." She smiled up into his eyes.

Juli ducked her head to keep from laughing. Like the Royal Canadian Mounted Police, Amy Hilton always got her man. Brett didn't look any happier than prisoners captured by the RCMP in old-time northern adventure stories!

That night's news took the focus off the proposed outing. Another bank had been hit in broad daylight. Same lone figure. Same clothing. Same note. Yet one major difference set the police force cheering: An unsuspecting customer had walked into the bank just after the robbery. She nearly bumped into the thief, who was on his way out. Although she only got a glimpse of him, the customer felt she might possibly be able to recognize the man!

"I wish the news hadn't said that," Juli whispered. "She might be in danger."

"Don't worry," Dad reassured. "The police will make sure she's all right." Yet the wrinkle between his eyebrows betrayed concern as deep as Juli's.

CHAPTER 14

Amy Hilton stepped to the mirror in the hall of her home and smiled at the pretty blond confidently looking back. Her new designer jeans and jacket outfit, worn over a white shirt, had cost 'a leg and an arm,' as Shannon Riley would say. It was worth it. The soft fabric tinted Amy's eyes a true forget-me-not blue.

She blew her reflection a kiss, then jumped when a broadly grinning male face appeared in the mirror beside her own. Amy whirled and put her hands on her hips. "What's the big idea, creeping up on me?"

Her twin brother Ted snorted, "Creep? In a cast? Get real. If you hadn't been so busy admiring yourself, you'd have heard me clumping along." His mouth turned down. "Fat chance I have of doing any hiking, with this thing on my leg."

The new appreciation of her brother since his accident silenced Amy's automatic protest at his needling her. "At least you get to go."

"Yeah. Nice of Shannon's dad to let Mr. Scott drive the van so I'll have room for my cast. I also appreciate Juli's dad and Shannon waiting around until I saw Dr. Marlowe this morning." Ted thumped the cast. "The doctor cleared me to go, as long as I'm careful." He glanced at the clock. "It's 9:30. They'll be here soon. Brett's due at ten. We'll wait if you want to ride with us."

"Fat chance," Amy mimicked. "Not after I wangled it so I could be with him all the way to the mountains and back." She turned to the mirror again.

"He doesn't care about you," Ted said bluntly. Angry color flashed across his sister's face and he added, "Or Shannon. Or Molly. Or Juli. The only person Brett Jones really cares about is Brett Jones. Number One. *Numero uno.*"

Amy giggled. "I know. That and his precious white Mustang."

"So how come you hang around him like deer at a salt lick?" Ted demanded.

"Why not?" Not quite satisfied with her appearance, Amy continued to inspect her face and hair. "I like having a date, even on youth activities."

"You are cold-blooded," Ted accused. "I thought you liked the guy."

Amy dropped her pose. "I do. I'm also smart enough to know Brett Jones won't be hanging around with high school kids now that he's graduated. He let slip the other day he'd probably be moving on. It's been fun while it lasted."

"Oh? You wouldn't talk like this if it were Dave Gilmore, would you?"

Amy bit her lip to hide the stab of pain she felt inside at mention of the tall basketball player. For a fleeting moment unhappiness showed in her eyes. She knew Ted noticed by his expression in the mirror and the awkward way he thumped her shoulder and said, "Sorry. It's none of my business."

"No, it isn't." She tossed her head. "Besides, Dave Gilmore's just a guy."

"See that you remember it." Ted hugged her and grinned. "I'm just glad you aren't crazy about Brett Jones. I've tried to like him, but somehow—"

"Shhh," Amy warned. "There's the doorbell." She ran down the hall with the speed and grace that came from cheerleading. "Hi, Shannon. Ted's all ready." She waved to Gary Scott. "See you soon." Amy watched the van move out of sight, half wishing she'd agreed to ride with her twin. Their earlier conversation had rubbed some of the sparkle off the day. Besides, if Brett were in one of his moods, she'd have had a lot more fun in a group.

Amy sighed. Too late to do anything about it now. Ted might suspect his sister liked Dave Gilmore, but no one else must know. So what if handsome Brett Jones and his classic Mustang couldn't compare with Dave's laughing eyes and mischievous smile? She shrugged and lightly hummed,

"When I'm Not Near the Girl I Love," a song from the musical *Finian's Rainbow*. She paraphrased the last words and defiantly sang, "I'll impress the boy I'm near!"

The absurd thought tilted her mouth into a smile. It broadened when Brett arrived, bubbling over with good spirits. Amy climbed into the bucket seat, determined to be so bewitching he couldn't help admiring her. His dark eyes shone when she chattered on about his car, immaculate inside and out.

Brett's sudden stillness turned Amy's attention from the North Fork of the Nooksack River they had been following. He looked like he hated her. The next instant he became his usual attractive self. Had she imagined it? She must have. Yet she couldn't quite forget, although Brett turned on the charm for the rest of the drive. He also proved so attentive, Amy saw several of the group glance at him in amazement. Brett acted like she was the greatest invention since pizza.

The youth group had brought the grandfather of all picnics. After they stuffed themselves, Amy rounded the van to get Ted's windbreaker. Her denim jacket had proved too warm for hiking. Brett Jones stood facing her, with Juli Scott close in his arms. Too stunned to move, Amy watched Brett bend his head and kiss the struggling girl. "I'm crazy about you," he muttered when she tore free.

"You're crazy, period!" Juli scrubbed hard at her lips with her hand.

Brett's face became a thundercloud. He took a menacing step toward Juli.

Courage she hadn't known she possessed lent strength to Amy's paralyzed feet. She ran to the angry couple. Juli whipped toward her. The disgust in her face declared the truth. *Play it cool,* a little voice inside Amy warned. "Was it that bad, Juli? Here." She fished in her pocket and handed over a tissue. Proud of herself and the way she had handled things, Amy brushed past Brett. She unhurriedly took Ted's windbreaker from the van, then marched off with her head held high. She didn't know where she was going. She didn't care. She only knew she had to get away before she screamed, bawled, or did both.

Juli shifted her gaze from Amy's rigid, retreating back. "You creep! If you ever touch me again, you'll be sorry!" More upset than she had been in months, and not trusting herself to be around the others, Juli climbed into the van and slammed the doors. She saw Brett shrug, raise a dark eyebrow, and walk to the youth group. He called, "All right, you hikers. Who's ready to move out?"

A fresh pot of anger boiled. It took several minutes of talking with God for Juli to get enough control to join the crowd. She hid her feelings by a pretense of excitement over the hike. She kept up the gaiety on the trail, all the while wondering where Amy was and admiring the way the tiny blond had handled things.

"Where's Amy?" someone asked.

Juli gritted her teeth, but Brett laughed. "We had a fight. She flounced off. Probably watched us leave. She'll be back with Ted when we return from our hike. Right, Juli?" He had the audacity to smile, as if they shared a secret.

She wouldn't give him the satisfaction of knowing that if she weren't a Christian, a certain Juli Scott would love to rearrange one Brett Jones's treacherous face. "I wouldn't know." She turned her back on him and hiked doggedly up the trail. For what seemed like endless hours, she kept up her role-playing, but pretense changed to concern when they returned and found Amy wasn't with Ted.

"It's my fault. I'll go find her," Brett offered. Without waiting for anyone to volunteer to go with him, he took off in long strides. An hour later he returned, raging like the Nooksack in flood. When Ted asked if he had found Amy, Brett yelled, "I found her all right. We had the fight to end all fights. I'm sick of her jealousy and tantrums every time I look at another girl." He ignored the shocked silence, flung himself into his car, and threw gravel when he wildly took off.

"Something fishy here," Gary Scott said, turning to face the group. "Kareem, Dave, Shannon, and Juli, come with me. The rest of you stay here, please. If Amy is as upset as Brett says, she won't want the whole group coming after her." He headed off quickly in the direction from which Brett had moments earlier returned.

When Amy had fled from the unpleasant scene between Juli and Brett, she paid little attention to where she was going. Neither did she watch the faint trail she found and took. A little over a mile from the spot where the bus and van were parked, she stumbled over a half-hidden, mossy rock and fell heavily. Pain shot through her ankle. Had she broken it? No, for she could wiggle all her toes and turn her foot. Evidently she had only twisted it.

Amy tried to walk, but it hurt too much. She moaned and hopped on one foot to the shade of a nearby evergreen tree. She dropped to the needle-covered ground and prepared to wait. Sooner or later, someone would come.

It proved to be later. Much later. Amy had removed her hiking shoe and sock, but could do little else to soothe her injured ankle. She did fold Ted's windbreaker into a kind of pad so she could prop up her foot. The hours crept by. Amy became more aware of her surroundings. In spite of the pain, some of the peace of the place settled over her. She watched clouds form patterns, something she hadn't done for years. The warm air made her drowsy. She fell asleep to the hum of bees tipsy with pollen from a million wildflowers.

"Amy. Amy, where are you?" a voice called.

She opened sleepy eyes. "Here." It came out as a whisper. She tried again. An answering shout brought her to a sitting position. A few minutes later, a tall figure loomed over her and she stared straight up into Brett Jones's angry face.

"You are so stupid," he raged. "What are you doing here, anyway?"

"I fell and hurt myself." She pointed to the swollen, discolored ankle.

No sympathy lightened Brett's twisted face. "You've been nothing but trouble since the moment I first saw you. You and those friends of yours, always spying on me, calling me names. You deserve everything that's happened to you."

Amy couldn't believe the change in his face. "You *are* crazy, just like Juli said," she cried. A sudden move of her foot brought a rush of tears. "You must have a guilty conscience about something or you wouldn't be so paranoid!"

Brett raised one hand. For a moment, Amy thought he was going to hit her. Instead, he turned on his heel and pelted back down the trail. She started to call out, then shook her head. "Please send someone else, God," she whispered. "Something is terribly wrong with Brett. I'm afraid of him." She sank back to a lying position. Again peace flowed through her, along with an awareness of God's love.

A short time later, the rescue party arrived. Before they started back Gary Scott said, "If you can hang in there a few minutes more, I need to know everything that happened after you left the group, while it's fresh in your mind."

"All right." She repeated the events and conversation. "Brett acted wild, like he was going totally out of control. I even thought he was going to hit me."

Gary made notes in a small pad and tucked them in his pocket. "Thanks. Let's get you home; you'll need to ride in the van. I don't believe your date waited for you."

"I hope not. If I never see Brett again, it will be a life-time too soon!"

Juli whispered to Dad, "May Dave and I ride home in the van?"

"Sorry," he told her. "I want Amy to lie down and be quiet. Ted with his cast needs extra space, too." He added, "By the time you and Dave get there, I'll have Andrew and Mary Payne on hand. We may be able to clear up some things." He looked as if he wanted to say more, but closed his lips in the way that meant, *No questions, please.* Juli knew better than to push it.

All the way home on the bus, Dave and Juli talked quietly. A million suspicions came to mind. Most didn't fit. "Like crooked puzzle pieces." Juli sighed. "I hope somebody starts putting them together soon!"

"Brett turned out to be a real fake, didn't he?"

"Yes." Why should the innocent question make Juli's nerves quiver like guitar strings? Or make her feel she stood behind a thin curtain that hid the truth? The feeling stayed with her all the way to the church and back home in Dave's Mustang. Yet no matter how hard she concentrated, she could not figure it out.

When Juli and Dave arrived, they found Shannon, her father, and the Paynes gathered in the comfortable, wood-paneled living room. Andrew took charge, his face serious beneath brick-colored hair. "FBI agents aren't notorious for sharing information," he began. "In this case, and it definitely is a case, you're all involved in one way or another." He grinned at them.

"You've shown yourselves to be trustworthy. We know what you hear in this room will go no further. Here's the picture. Even before Mary and I talked with you earlier, we'd been assigned to investigate the Bellingham robberies. They would normally fall under local jurisdiction. However, there has been a wave of holdups, some violent, across the western United States. Authorities called in the FBI to see if they are related. It appears they aren't."

"I don't understand," Shannon faltered. "What does this have to do with Brett?" Her eyes looked enormous. "You don't think *he* robbed the banks!"

Andrew raised a reddish eyebrow. "He's been picked up for questioning."

Juli felt the color drain from her face. "That's it!" Seven shocked faces turned toward her. She breathlessly rushed on. "Dad, will you please read what Amy told us Brett said?"

"Of course." He took the notepad from his pocket and read Amy's statement: " 'You've been nothing but trouble since the moment I first saw you. You and those friends of yours, always spying on me, calling me names. You deserve everything that's happened to you.' "

"Why would he say such a thing?" Dave protested. "The first time Brett saw Amy or any of us was when he showed up at Sunday school class. We treated him great. Kareem even had him play the victim in the Good

Samaritan skit."

Juli looked at Andrew. He grinned, nodded, and said, "Go ahead."

She had the feeling he knew what she intended to say. "Brett's no victim," she announced. "What if church wasn't the first time he saw us? Remember how sure Amy was that the white Mustang she drooled over at Pizza Palace was the same car he had at church? She insisted, even when he said it wasn't. That's not all." Juli took a deep breath, closed her eyes to get it right, then opened them and said, "Remember when someone lurched into Amy and she spilled pizza on Ted's letter jacket? He called out, 'Hey, watch where you're going.' Then Amy said really loud, 'It's not my fault *some guy* bumped me.' "

Excitement ran through the circle of friends like a charge of lightning.

"It can't be Brett," Shannon protested. "He received a warning note, just like the rest of us, even though he wasn't at the Pizza Palace!"

"He may have been," Andrew grimly corrected. "Stolen money and all. It's the oldest trick in the book for crooks to plant false clues. What better way to be in the clear than to appear to be a victim along with the rest of you?"

A telephone ring shattered the stunned silence. Gary Scott answered, then beckoned for Andrew. After a long time, the FBI agent came back. Juli couldn't tell by his face whether it was good news or bad. He finally spoke. "We've got our man. After the customer at the last bank robbery made a tentative identification, Jones cracked. Your friend Amy was right. The fear he had been seen became an obsession. He fought it by trying to intimidate anyone who witnessed him at the Pizza Palace that Wednesday."

"It's hard to believe an eighteen-year-old boy could do this," Anne Scott said.

"He's actually in his early twenties," Andrew informed them. "He falsified records in order to attend Hillcrest and find out who Juli and her friends were."

She shivered. "Was he the hit-and-run driver?"

"Yes. Unless he's lying, he only meant to scare Ted Hilton, not hit him. At least Jones had the decency to take his victim to the hospital."

"Did he do all those other things?" Shannon asked in a shaky voice.

The agent sighed. "Jones is a funny kind of crook. He admitted slashing Amy's tires, but grew furious when asked why he didn't trash the rest of the car. Said he'd never do that to a great car like a Mustang! He followed John and Molly, but claims he just wanted to scare them. Ditto for the footprints under the Rileys' window, the scratches around the keyhole on Dave's car, the warning notes. He also claims the gun he used to hold up the banks was never loaded."

"Sounds like a psycho," Mary Payne said.

"I'm so glad it's over," Juli cried. She had long suspected Brett Jones wasn't so wonderful. Yet it hurt to think anyone would come to church for the purpose of identifing possible witnesses to a crime he had planned and committed! Had anything Brett heard that day made the slightest difference? If convicted and given a prison sentence, would the memory of people who accepted him for what he said he was ever cross his mind? *I hope so, God,* she prayed. *You have the power to change lives and hearts. Please, help Brett realize he can be forgiven, and accept You as his Savior.*

"It isn't over yet," Andrew warned. "There's a good chance at least some of you will have to go to court and tell what you saw and heard."

Shannon looked frightened, but quickly said, "Well, the Bible says we all have trials and revelations." She looked surprised when everyone laughed.

"Trials and *tribulations,*" Juli said. She grinned at Shannon, who had joined in the laughter. "On the other hand, who knows? I have a feeling we may all be shocked at what revelations are made at Brett Jones's trial!"

Thursday Trials, Juli Scott Super Sleuth Book Four, is now available.

Juli Scott and friends from her church youth group are subpoenaed to appear in court as witnesses to a bank robbery case. Juli looks forward to it, believing it will be nothing more than good experience for the mystery books she plans to write. She is wrong.

Dave Gilmore, Juli's boyfriend *pro tem*, grins and shrugs. "Piece of cake. We're on the witness stand for maybe two minutes. We answer a couple of questions. We're out of there." Dave's in for the shock of his life.

Juli's best friend, Shannon Riley, who never quotes anything correctly, dreads what she calls "trials and revelations." Although she means trials and *tribulations,* Shannon is right. What should be a simple court appearance turns ugly. Doing the right thing also brings startling revelations —and sets Juli and her friends up for trouble from an unknown enemy seeking revenge.

Books for ages 7 to 12

Kid Stuff
Fun-filled Activity Books for ages 7-12

Bible Questions and Answers for Kids
Collection #1 and #2

Brain-teasing questions and answers from the Bible are sure to satisfy the curiosity of any kid. And fun illustrations combined with Bible trivia make for great entertainment and learning! Trade paper; 8 ½" x 11" $2.97 each.

Bible Crosswords for Kids
Collection #1 and #2

Two great collections of Bible-based crossword puzzles are sure to challenge kids ages seven to twelve. Hours of enjoyment and Bible learning are combined into these terrific activity books. Trade paper; 8 ½" x 11" $2.97 each.

The Kid's Book of Awesome Bible Activities
Collection #1 and #2

These fun-filled, Bible-based activity books include challenging word searches, puzzles, hidden pictures, and more! Bible learning becomes fun and meaningful with *The Kid's Book of Awesome Bible Activities*. Trade paper; 8 ½" x 11" $2.97 each.

Available wherever books are sold.
Or order from:
Barbour Publishing, Inc.
P.O. Box 719
Uhrichsville, Ohio 44683
http://www.barbourbooks.com

If you order by mail, add $2.00 to your order for shipping. Prices subject to change without notice.